The Hunting
of Wilberforce Pike

Wilberforce Pike is a cruel, red-whiskered, cat-thief, who snatches unsuspecting felines to be made into fur coats. Oliver Simpkin, a previously sheltered pet, is one of Pike's first captives, but the fearless Power Station gang comes to his rescue and saves his skin. He joins them in the mysterious cat underworld and swears to bring revenge on the villain Pike and his equally sinister wife. And so the mad chase begins

. . .
This is an extremely funny book, with a strong, adventurous story-line, for readers of ten upwards.

'A refreshing and hilarious story with some un-forgettable characters.'　　　*Eastern Daily Mail*

The Hunting of Wilberforce Pike

MOLLY LEFEBURE

Illustrated by A. Wainwright

COLLINS · LIONS

First published 1970 by Victor Gollancz Ltd
First published in Lions 1975
by William Collins Sons and Co Ltd
14 St James's Place, London SW1

© Molly Lefebure 1970
Illustrations © A. Wainwright 1970

Printed in Great Britain
by William Collins Sons and Co Ltd, Glasgow

For Natasha

Contents

1. Short, if not all Sweet

Oliver Simpkin was at the awkward age. He had suddenly changed from a cuddly snowball of a kitten, adored by the whole family, into a skimpy, leggy troublemaker.

His intentions were of the best. Every morning he said to himself, 'I am going to be good today,' but within minutes he was in disgrace. Perhaps, eager to catch a fly, he climbed the new curtains in the dining-room, or he knocked over a milk-bottle on the doorstep, or fell head-first into the coke-hod, or made a very small mess in a deserted shoe. Little things, but they mounted up.

'That wretched animal, he'll send me demented!' gasped poor Mrs Robinson, the mother of the family to whom Oliver belonged. 'As if I hadn't enough to do, without a kitten causing endless mischief!'

She placed a dish of something yellow and nice-smelling on the kitchen-table, then she went out of the room. Oliver crept in unnoticed and jumped on to a chair and from thence on to the table, to get a better look. Steam rose from the dish. Cautiously, Oliver crept across the table, which had a white, slippery surface. He crouched by the dish, watching the steam (which puzzled him) and sniffing the nice smell. Then he raised himself a little and craned forward, very slowly and carefully, his tongue curling out in excitement and interest. At that moment he heard a loud screech behind him, which made him jump; his paws shot from under him, skidding on the table top, and he fell head-first into the yellow stuff. The dish tipped up, hit him between the eyes and sent him flying through the air, to land hard on the floor, while the voice screamed, 'My custard! My custard!' He glimpsed Mrs Robinson looming over him, wailing and waving her arms; then she snatched up the broom and with it she swept Oliver out of the kitchen, head-over-heels down the steps into the garden. Then she slammed the door.

Oliver, soused in custard, sore from the bristly broom and feeling all in little bits, picked himself up gingerly. He could hear someone laughing in a nasty sort of way. He knew, without looking, that it was the blackbird.

This blackbird was the bane of Oliver's life. The Robinsons lived in a roomy house with a large garden which was the home of a vast tribe of blackbirds, headed by a fierce patriarch who was convinced that he owned the garden, the house and the Robinsons included. The bird stood no truck from Oliver, whom he bullied, chivvied, scolded and teased every time the poor young cat so much as ventured a whisker out of doors.

Now this blackbird, perched on a stump only a few feet from Oliver, rocked back and forth with laughter.

'Ho ho ho! you don't half look a sight! What a mess you're in!' chortled the blackbird. 'And what a purler you took down those steps! Talk about head-first! The way she threw you out; my giddy aunt! Wonder she didn't shove you in the dustbin while she was about it!'

Oliver, too shaken by his fall to speak, turned his back on the blackbird and began licking himself clean. The impudent bird hopped to within inches of him and appeared eager to jab him with a very sharp bright bill.

'Ho ho ho! Talk about a mess! You look a sight, you really do!'

'Shut up!'

'Way you went head-first down those steps! Ho ho ho!'

'I hope that that Mr Tyler comes along and eats you!' bawled Oliver, infuriated. 'Come to that, I'll eat you myself one of these days!'

'You, my young shaver!' jeered the blackbird. 'You couldn't catch a fly, let alone me!'

'You wait till Mr Tyler comes along; you'll snigger the other side of your silly beak then!'

'Poo, that Tyler!' sneered the blackbird. 'I'll give him what-for if he comes walking in my garden!'

Mr Tyler was a large, lean, keen-eyed, silent-footed tom who lived in a house in a neighbouring street and treated the surrounding area, including at least a dozen back-gardens, as his exclusive territory, or 'manor' as he called it. A mysterious

8

animal, he was often absent from home, re-appearing suddenly, when least expected. Any tom-cat caught trespassing within Tyler's domain was chased off without ceremony; lady cats vanished discreetly into the bushes at his approach. It was said that he had torn more ears off rival toms than any other cat in the district. Oliver was frankly terrified of him and always fled at the first, distant glimpse of him. Even Mr Tyler, however, balked at a scrap with the celebrated blackbird.

Brooding over the injustice of the custard episode and the mockery of the blackbird, Oliver retired to the shrubbery. Here he caught and killed a mouse. Very proud of this, and hoping to create a good impression by his cleverness, Oliver carried the mouse into the kitchen to show Mrs Robinson. She screamed and chased him out with a wet mop. He found himself yet once again somersaulting down the garden steps; the inevitable blackbird's sniggering came from the bushes.

Thus, Oliver blundered from one mishap to the next.

The days shortened as mellow autumn dwindled into winter; soon the evenings were twilit at an early hour. Oliver loved the excitement of a garden so thrillingly different from the place that he knew in the daylight, but the Robinsons irked him by fetching him indoors before it became really dusky. 'You'll make the wrong sort of friends and pick up fleas if you play outside after dark,' said little Lucy Robinson as she carried him into the house.

'He's a pedigree cat; he mustn't be allowed to turn into a scruffy roamer,' said Mrs Robinson. 'Besides, if he starts wandering at night a cat-thief may get him.'

Oliver had a good private laugh over this one. Cat-thief. What a bogey tale!

So, in spite of these warnings, Oliver sneaked out after supper to play in the twilight whenever he could. The young cat explored the pools of shadow under the shrubs, the dark corridors between the trees and the garden walls, the secret recesses of the michaelmas-daisy groves. He danced gaily over the lawn, patched and striped with light cast from uncurtained windows. He became enslaved by the full moon which, floating vast and silver like a never-to-be-reached giant platter of

9

cream, sent shining tingles of desire shivering through him and he dreamed of reaching the moon and licking a big hole in it and licking on and on until he came to the other side. He loved this dream very much.

As winter drew nearer the evenings became foggy; curtains of mist hung between the trees, shadows swam about in shoals. In this mysterious landscape unseen things darted and rustled, luring Oliver farther and farther afield: the nextdoor garden and the next, the garden next to that, and the garden beyond. As he became bolder Oliver took to exploring front-gardens

too; crouching on top of gateposts, watching the eerie emptinesses of the night-time streets. The Robinsons often had to call him for a long while before he came in; they made it clear that they disapproved strongly of his new habits. But Oliver was convinced that he was grown-up enough and clever enough to take care of himself; his ambition was to reach full tom's estate and to stay out all night.

One murky evening, as he sat in the shadows of a privet-hedged passageway studying noises, a footfall, a dry leaf scratching, a gate sighing, Oliver suddenly noticed a long, furry, tail-like something whisking on the ground a few feet from him. He stared at it in fascination. Now it twitched, now lay still, now it rippled and flickered, now lay still again. Oliver began stealing cautiously forward; the tail lay motionless, then twisted so excitingly that Oliver stiffened to pounce. A second or so of again lying still and the thing moved once more. Oliver darted forward, patting swiftly at it with his paw. He poised over it, playing raptly with it, quite unable to decide what it was, but finding it wonderful fun and apparently harmless. Could he catch it? Or could he not? Now he thought he had it, now he hadn't. He had never met with a more intriguing object in his life.

Suddenly a hard, huge hand grasped the scruff of his neck. He was lifted quickly and thrust head-first into a sack. Whoever it was that had caught him then walked off with him, fast.

2. At Home with Wilberforce Pike

'There y'are, Puss, into your basket,' said a rough, hairy voice. Oliver, terrified, found himself being tipped out of the sack into a smelly, battered cat-basket. He had no sooner landed in the basket than he tried to jump out, but the lid was fetched down hard on his head as the voice said, nastily, 'Oh no you don't; you're coming home with me!'

The basket was carried a farther short distance, then put on the ground. There was a small opening in one end of the basket; Oliver shifted round until he could peer out. There was nothing to see except two very big feet in rubber-soled shoes and part of the wheel of a van. The feet shuffled about a bit, a metal van-door swung open. Then Oliver's basket was raised and shoved into the van and the metal door was slammed shut with a clang, which set Oliver all a-quiver. He could hear desperate, panicky cats mewing near at hand. Pressed against the tiny window of the basket alongside him he glimpsed a frantic little face; then the van started up with a jolt and the journey was too dark, noisy and stuffy for Oliver to do anything but huddle petrified in his basket, gasping for air.

At last the van drew to a standstill. There was much banging about, thumping and stamping, the rough hairy voice muttering unpleasantly at intervals, against a background of mewing cats. Oliver felt his basket once more being raised and carried; up some stairs, he thought. Then it was slung down, hard. There was a perfect cat-chorus going on around him and an animal smell solid enough to slice with a knife.

A dialogue started between the rough voice and another; this a woman's voice, almost as unpleasant as the man's.

'Got a good haul this evening, Pikey?' asked the lady.

'Haul's the word for it orright. Come on, gimme a hand gettin' these perishin' cats in their cages. Now, which one'll we decant first? That nasty-looking tabby there; might as well.

Cor, blimey, talons on 'im like a perishin' tiger! If he ain't a savage, my name's not Wilberforce Pike!'

Then followed a session of confused noises: the spitting, snarling and yowling of a furious cat, the rattling of a cage, the cries of Mr and Mrs Wilberforce Pike as they struggled with the tabby. At last he was got into a cage and the Pikes turned their attention to the next victim. Wilberforce sounded happier with this one.

'Cor, nice little lady cat. There, ain't she sweet? What's yer name, duck?'

'Get on with it, Pikey. Cage her quick, before she gets fed up and starts scratching.'

'She won't scratch; will yer, little gal? You wouldn't scratch yer Uncle Wilberforce . . .' There was a loud spitting sound, followed without pause by a yelp from Mr Pike. 'Blimey, spat right in me eye!'

Mrs Pike gave a high cackle of laughter. 'Don't say I didn't warn you!'

'No manners, she ain't got,' said Mr Pike. 'Still, who needs manners when they're gonna finish as a fun-fur? Now, wot we got here?'

He unfastened Oliver's basket and raised the lid. Oliver sat up slowly, blinking; dazzled by the glare from a naked light bulb dangling from the dirty ceiling. A huge red round face, topped by a gleaming bald head, presented itself a few feet from the astounded cat. On either side of this face stuck out an enormous purple ear, each with a network of tiny, but distinct violet veins over it, and carroty bristles of hair sprouting from within it. More tufts of carroty hair grew, brush-like, above these ears. The rest of the man's features were equally nasty; a mouth with loose, wet lips and dirty broken teeth; a squashy-looking nose and small, pale blue eyes under carroty, very bushy overhanging eyebrows. This unsavoury person had a grubby old green scarf round his throat, upon the folds of which rested a stubbly double chin.

Oliver stared in dreadful fascination. Wilberforce Pike stared back. At last he said, 'He's no cat. He's a bloomin' owl!'

'Never did like white cats meself. Creepy,' said Mrs Pike.

Oliver now turned his head to look at her. She was small, just as dirty as her husband, with frizzy grey hair like old wire wool, and heavy black rings round her eyes; Oliver thought to himself that, if anyone looked like an owl, she did.

'Cats white, homes bright. Gospo,' said Wilberforce. 'Gospo. That's what we'll call this one, Gospo.'

'I'll give you Gospo!' gasped Oliver, jutting out his claws and kicking; but Wilberforce had him bundled into a small, filthy cage before the angry young cat could do much damage.

There were five cats transferred from baskets to cages: the savage tabby who had given the Pikes so much trouble; the little lady who spat; Oliver; a young black cat of much the same age as Oliver, and an abyssinian. Three other cats, a brindle, a tortoiseshell-and-white, and an aristocratic blue persian, were already caged; obviously prisoners of somewhat longer standing.

'There we are, Mrs P.,' said Wilberforce with satisfaction, as he finally caged the abyssinian, who was almost as troublesome as the tabby had been, 'how's that for a night's work?'

'Lovely,' said his lady. 'Eight nice cat skins, all lined up.'

'Hides, my dear, not cat skins. Please call them hides,' urged Wilberforce. 'Hides for fun-furs. A much higher-class trade altogether, my dear, from dealing in cat skins.'

'Makes no difference,' said Mrs Pike. 'It's all cat and there's no getting away from it, whatever you call it.'

'Five in one evening,' sighed Wilberforce contentedly. 'Very nice going. Only need four more pussies and that'll make a round dozen to sell. And now, my love, you can go and get my supper ready.'

The imprisoned cats, left to themselves, stared about them with wide night-peering eyes (Wilberforce had frugally switched out the light before going downstairs to his supper). Oliver's first thoughts were of escape, now that their captor was gone; his gaze turned automatically to the window. It was small, tightly shut, with a faded, torn pink curtain partly drawn across it; one pane of glass was badly cracked but over this had been strongly gummed a sheet of thick brown paper. Moreover, what was the point of Oliver thinking of possible escape

14

through the window when he had first to get out of his cage? The cats' cages were most securely fastened.

Forlornly, Oliver let his eyes roam over the rest of the room, which was very cold and stank abominably. Chipped and broken lino covered the floor; from the walls old gravy-coloured paper was peeling off in strips. There was no furniture apart from the trestles upon which the cages stood and one lop-sided wooden chair. Several cat-baskets were stowed untidily on the floor beneath the trestles. From a peg on the back of the door dangled a long, furry tail-like something which Oliver stared hard at, certain that he had seen it somewhere before, but unable to place it.

At last the abyssinian said, 'I wonder what he means to do with us?'

'Why, just what he said; fur coats,' replied the tortoise-shell-and-white cat. 'We're gonna end up being worn by some human being as a nice smart outfit.'

At this the young black cat began to cry very hard indeed and the little lady cat hid her face in her paws and sobbed, while even Oliver felt a furtive tear or two steal down his cheeks. He would have liked to have been awfully brave, but suddenly it seemed very difficult.

'Humans are a cruel, wicked lot,' said the brindle. 'And as ignorant as they're cruel and wicked. They've been taught that the world belongs to them; taught that they're higher, somehow, than the rest of us animals. We're living creatures, same as them, and all born into the same world, but they think that they have a better right to live in it than the rest of creation. Kill us for food, kill us because they want to wear our coats, kill us for fun. Kill us all clean off the face of the earth if they want; they're certain it's their right.'

'I want to go home!' wept the young black cat. 'Oh, can't someone get me out of here! I want to go home!' And he broke down completely, huddled hopelessly behind the bars of his cage, while the little lady cat (who was more kitten than cat and, truth to tell, didn't look that much of a lady) sobbed loudly and screwed her grimy paws into her eyes, and Oliver too shed open tears of despair.

'Well, strike me, I never saw such a lot for waterworks,'

said the savage tabby, speaking for the first time. 'Ain't none of you lot got no fight in yer?'

'Fight?' wailed the abyssinian. 'How can we fight? We're all caged up. We haven't got a chance to fight or escape or anything!'

'Come on,' said the tabby, 'never say die. It's old Pikey wot'll end up a fun-fur, just you see; 'im and his red sprouts behind his ears. Red-sprouting fun-fur, that's how he'll end up, and that's a promise, sure as my name's Nosher.'

'Brave talk,' said the brindle. 'But exactly *how* are you going to turn him into a red-sprouting fun-fur?'

'Once we're outa here, mate, I'll settle him; just you see,' said Nosher.

'And tell me, Mr Nosher,' said the abyssinian, 'how are you proposing to get us out of here?'

'Don't you worry,' replied Nosher. 'My mates'll rescue us.'

'Which mates?' asked the brindle.

'Guv'nor Goofer and his Power Station cats. Well known gang, that lot is. Real good gang and all,' boasted Nosher. 'Live with the gang at the Power Station, I do. Real good times we have, too.'

'What's a Power Station?' asked the little lady cat.

'A Power Station is where they generate electricity,' said the brindle. He was one of those animals who always knows everything.

'And the reason us lot all went there was because we was strays and had nowhere else to go, so one by one we finished up there,' resumed Nosher. 'It's a real good pad, too; nice an' warm, plenty of grub, loads of company. Cor, stone it, I bet old Buckingham Palace ain't better! You can always count on a good rat-hunt, too.'

The cats, all very impressed by this, but trying not to show it, stared at him in wide-eyed silence. Nosher continued, 'This old Power Station, it's down by the river, see, and there's gardens by the river, and that's where the rats live. And if it wasn't for us cats, I tell you straight, them rats would take over the Power Station.'

'What size rats?' asked the brindle.

'King-sized, mate, king-sized,' boasted Nosher, in his element. 'Whole army of 'em, and the old man rat what leads 'em, he's big as you are.'

'Oo! I wouldn't wanna meet him!' squealed the little lady cat.

'Real evil lookin' beast he is,' said Nosher. 'Got only one eye, with a black patch over. Lost the other, fightin'. And he wears a red bow on his tail. Proud as punch he is of his bloomin' tail. Squeals, his name is, General Squeals. And he's got an 'orrible lookin' Sergeant called Fleaby; he's got whacking great yellow teeth what stick out coupla inches afront of his face, old Fleaby has.'

'D'you f-fight them?' asked the young black cat, shuddering.

'Us Power Station lot'll fight anything,' replied Nosher magnificently.

'I'm a stray too,' said the little lady cat. 'Only thing I know 'bout me is I'm called Selina an' I used to belong to a fam'ly wot went off to Australia and left me behind; people up and down the street feed me and I sleep rough in sheds and that. I was with a nice lady a little while back, her and her husband, ever so nice they was; not married long. They took me in and was ever so kind to me; give me this collar I'm wearing.' She raised a paw and proudly indicated a tatty little plastic collar studded with imitation diamonds. 'But then they went and got a baby; where from I don't know, and what for I can't think, and after that they went right off me; all they thought about was the blooming baby. So I took to living rough again. I can manage!'

And with a toss of her head she briskly opened a small plastic handbag, took out a chipped compact and started powdering her nose with a very dirty powder-puff. Then she licked her paw and brushed her eyebrows and whiskers, peering at herself meanwhile in the cracked mirror of the compact. She was dingy black and very furry, with huge round amber eyes and sharply pointed little ears pricked upright amidst a complicated *coiffure* of heavy back-combed fringe that made her look very much like a gollywog. Grubby, indeed downright scruffy, nonetheless the young lady obviously fancied herself. 'Well,' observed the brindle sarcastically, after he

17

had watched Selina powder her nose, titivate her eyebrows and pat out her fringe, 'this is doubtless an interesting interlude, but while we're talking and prinking ourselves time is running short. If that Wilberforce Pike catches four more cats tomorrow night he'll sell the lot of us next day. And that will be the end of us! So these wonderful mates of yours had better work fast to rescue us, Mr Nosher!'

'All in good time, all in good time,' said Nosher. 'Give 'em a chance to find us.'

'Exactly,' said the abyssinian. 'Nobody knows where we are; that horrible man has driven us to the other side of the town. What chance has anyone of finding us?' And he began to wail so miserably that in an instant he had all the other cats wailing too, with the exception of Nosher, who was thoroughly disgusted by the company.

'Blimey!' snarled he, 'what a collection of weeping-willows! Talk about making fun-furs, you lot's more suitable for making raincoats! Look 'ere, we got to keep our spirits up. Waterworks never did no good, I can tell you that for a start. Waterworks never got nobody nowhere.'

'True,' gulped the tortoiseshell-and-white, 'but at the same time you can hardly expect us to be cheerful.'

'What we got to do is make a non-stop racket calling for help,' said Nosher. 'Take turns kicking up a real old rumpus. Some cat or other in the neighbourhood is sure to hear us and pass the word along the cat-vine. But first let's introduce ourselves to one another, like, so's we know who we all are. Then, that done, we'll get a real good noise on the go.'

The brindle said that his name was Albert and he belonged to a school caretaker. The tortoiseshell-and-white introduced himself as Binns, the abyssinian said that he was called Leo and lived with an artist, the persian cat refused to introduce herself, while Selina had already done so. Nosher then turned to Oliver with a friendly grin, 'Now young fella, what do they call you at home, eh?'

'Oliver Simpkin, please sir,' replied Oliver, shyly.

'Well then, you stop snivelling, Oliver, and keep smiling and you'll be orright,' said Nosher. He turned to the young black cat. 'And your name, waterworks?'

The young black cat replied, chokingly, 'Sebastian.'

'Cor blimey, the names people give their cats these days,' said Nosher. 'Sebastian, eh? Well, Sebastian, and where d'you come from?'

'I belong to Miss P-Pringle,' said Sebastian. And then he started crying again. 'Oh, I do want to g-go home!'

'He's not much cop,' said Nosher, eyeing Sebastian in disgust. 'When I was his age I'da bin downright ashamed to be

seen boo-hooing like that in public, straight I would. Come on Sebastian, give over the wanna-go-home and start helping us get a rescue.'

The cats divided into three groups: the abyssinian and Oliver; Binns, Selina and Sebastian; Albert and Nosher. The persian still refused to have anything to do with the other cats and remained seated with her back to them, staring hard at an imaginary fly on the ceiling of her cage.

The three groups took it in turn to mew for help; at intervals Nosher signalled to them to stop and listen. They hoped to hear some cat's reply, outside in the dark, but not a sound reached them. At one point they did attract attention; but not the kind that they wanted. The door opened; there was a dreadful bellow of, 'Shurrup!' from Wilberforce and an old boot whizzed across the room, noisily striking against the bars of Albert's cage and falling to the ground with a heavy thud. Wilberforce slammed the door shut; they heard him shambling off; he was wearing slippers. For a while the cats sat in utter silence, staring disdainfully at the boot; then Nosher gave them another signal and all eight of them began mewing in unison. Even the persian had changed her mind and was calling, 'Help!' with the rest. But no help came.

3. Scratch, the Greatest

The cats called all night; by next morning they were quite hoarse. In spite of this they continued to mew, but no rescuers appeared. At mid-morning Mrs Pike, hideous in metal curlers and a dressing-gown, arrived to feed them small portions of milk and fish. The cats, by this time ravenous, gulped down these rations in a trice; they hoped for more, but no more was forthcoming. Mrs Pike vanished again. The weary hours dragged on.

Outside the day had become foggy; it grew dark early. Wilberforce came in to collect the cat-baskets, he also took with him the furry, tail-like object which dangled from the peg on the back of the door. Oliver, watching him take this, suddenly understood many things. The cat-thief then departed; they heard his van driving off.

'If he catches another four tonight, we're done for,' said Bins. 'Unless your mates turn up, Nosher, and they don't seem in any hurry to come.'

'How could they be expected to find us? Like looking for a needle in a haystack,' said the abyssinian.

'Keep smilin', they'll turn up, or my name ain't Nosher,' declared that animal, for the umpteenth time. 'Although my mates may turn up late, you needn't fear, for they'll appear.'

'Well I jolly well hope so, for all our sakes,' responded Albert. 'The sands of time are running out.'

'I will agree without a doubt, the sands of time are running out, but you'll all see that in the nick of time we shall be rescued quick,' rattled off Nosher.

This brought squeals of admiration from Selina. 'Ooh, in'ee clever? Makes up po'try easy as other chaps just talk!'

'When once you know the way to do it, you'll find there's really nothing to it,' responded Nosher, airily.

'Anybody can talk in rhyme if they want,' growled Albert.

'Let's hear you do it, then,' said Selina, challengingly.

'All right,' said Albert.

'Well, come on then. Start.'

'All very well to say "start",' said Albert. 'Give a cat a minute to think.'

'But old Nosh, he don't need no time to think. Just rattles it off,' said Selina.

'Anyone can *rattle*,' retorted Albert. 'It's when there's thought behind it that it counts.' He tilted his head a little and rolled his eyes up: evidently he was thinking. There was a lengthy pause. Selina, tittering, said at last, 'Get a move on, mister; we're all waiting.'

'It's a very long wait, for the brains of this mate, to make up a verse, for better or worse,' announced Nosher. Albert was furious. 'Now you've put me right off.'

'Oh, come on Albert,' said Binns. Everyone else chimed in, 'Yes, come on Albert!'

'My train of thought has been broken,' snarled Albert, much put out. 'My sort of poetry doesn't come like . . . like tooth-paste out of a tube: squish. It involves mental struggle.'

'Oh blimey, wish I hadn't asked!' giggled Selina.

'I must now insist upon at least five minutes' silence,' said Albert. Then he tilted his head on one side and rolled up his eyes again. There was another lengthy interval during which none of the cats uttered a sound: all stared at Albert.

In due course he opened his mouth wide, held it open for several seconds without saying anything, then began, 'Behold we number prisoners eight caught by the hand of wrathful fate . . .'

'What's that?' said Nosher, quickly.

'Please do not interrupt. If you don't know what wrathful fate is you can never have been to school. Now, I'll start again. "Behold we number prisoners eight caught by the hand of wrathful face . . ." There, you see; now you've put me clean off my stroke . . . "caught by the hand of wrathful *fate*, who has no mercy . . ." '

'Shut up!' snarled Nosher. 'I want to listen!'

'That doesn't make sense!' said the abyssinian. ' "Shut up, I

22

want to listen!" If Albert shuts up, how in the world can you listen to him?'

'Precisely,' said Albert. 'Moreover, I am not accustomed to being told to shut up by gutter-snipes. Or by anyone else for that matter. And now if you will have the goodness to stop interrupting me, I'll try again; for the third time. "Behold we number prisoners . . ." '

'Sssh!' hissed Sebastian.

'Words fail me,' said Albert. 'I've never met with such downright rudeness . . .'

There was the startlingly loud sound of a piece of paper splitting. The cats, as one, looked at the window: through both the now torn brown paper and a rent in the pink curtain was thrust a paw.

The paw waggled slowly up and down, sticking out its claws and drawing them in again. The cats watched, breathlessly. 'What is it?' asked Selina, scared. 'Oo, I don't like it!'

'It's the good old Guv'nor come to rescue us!' mewed Nosher in delight. 'I said my mates'd turn up; I said they would!'

The other cats, overwhelmingly excited, flung caution to the winds and began cheering. Rescued! Oliver felt tears once again rolling down his face; but this time they were tears of joy. 'Hooray!' he cried, half laughing, half crying. His companions were in a similarly emotional state. Only Albert retained sufficient control to utter a warning. 'Don't make so much row. We don't want to fetch Mrs Pike up with our noise.'

The cats became silent immediately. They glued their attention to the paw, which waved about some more. There were sounds of a person having an all-out battle with the brown paper; a second paw appeared, then the first paw was pulled back, then an entire leg emerged through the paper and the tear in the curtain and waved dementedly. Finally a whole cat heaved itself through the, by now, shredded brown paper and at once became hopelessly entangled in the pink curtain. A muffled voice said, 'You there, Nosh?'

Nosher, who was killing himself with silent laughter (and indeed if the moment had not been such a desperate one, all the cats would have laughed, for the Guv'nor's struggles were very funny to see) replied, 'Yeah; you got the right house any-way.'

'That you, Nosh?' repeated the smothered voice.

'Sure,' said Nosher. 'I said it's me.'

'Come and help me then!' gasped the Guv'nor. 'I'm caught; can't you see I'm caught?'

'I'm caught too, Guv,' said Nosher. 'Locked up in a flippin' cage.' To the other cats he observed, at large, 'Trust him to get hooked up in a blooming curtain. Real Guv'nor Goofer, he is.'

The Guv'nor kicked and struggled desperately. 'Can't anyone . . .'

'We're all locked up, mate. Else we'd come running,' said Nosher. 'Try to keep calm, Guv; easy does it.'

But the Guv'nor scorned this advice and continued to kick and struggle like crazy. Once he managed to peer through another hole in the curtain; he stared at the caged cats in amazement. 'Crumbs, you're all caged up!' he gasped.

'That's what I said!' mewed Nosher.

'Hang on, I'm coming,' said the Guv'nor, renewing his struggles. The words were barely out of his mouth when there was a hideous tearing noise. The curtain slowly split; the dis-traught Guv'nor, still hooked by one leg, descended head-first through the air, to be pulled up short with a jerk, dangling upside down, suspended spinning gently like a yo-yo at the end of its cord.

He was completely powerless; quite unable to free himself, absolutely strung up. He gave despairing mews and heaved and wriggled, while the other cats hissed advice, but it was no use. The only result of the Guv'nor's contortions was that he spun rather more: first clock-wise; then anti-clockwise. This process was repeated, then again repeated. 'I feel sick,' said the Guv'nor.

At that moment the cats heard the dread sound of Wilber-force Pike's van drawing up outside the house: the front door opened and shut, Pike's heavy footsteps came plodding up the stairs. Mrs Pike was asking him, 'How d'you get on, Pikey?' The cats, with baited breath, awaited his reply, 'Only three.'

Without the Guv'nor's presence this news would have meant that the cats had a temporary respite while Pike waited to catch his twelfth victim; as it was the words now spelled swift and certain doom. Barely ten minutes earlier the prisoners had been on the threshold of rescue and in raptures; now the horror of fun-furs loomed over them again, nearer than ever.

The door of the prison-chamber received a heavy kick from without and flew open; Wilberforce entered with a cat-basket under each arm. He stopped short, too astounded to speak, at the sight of the Guv'nor.

'Blimey!' he burst out at last. 'What have we here? A nice pussy come down from heaven! What a stroke of luck!'

'What's up?' asked Mrs Pike, following her husband into the room.

'Why, look 'ere. Pussy number twelve come to us of his own accord.'

Wilberforce put down the baskets and walked carefully towards the Guv'nor. Mrs Pike said, 'He must've jumped off the shed-roof clean through that bit of paper over the winder. Heard the other cats, I daresay. They ain't half been kicking up a rumpus.'

'Who says there's no such thing as Providence?' mused Wilberforce. 'Come just at the right time, he has, too. Now, where we gonna put him? Tell you what; he'll have to go in one of them full-sized cages, and we'll stow young Gospo, what's only a kitten, into that canary cage. It's only for one night. I'll sell 'em tomorrow.'

Without more ado Mr and Mrs Pike applied themselves to transferring Oliver to the canary cage. He was outraged. 'Canary cage! Only a kitten!' He began to spit even before they reached him. 'Mind out,' said Wilberforce. 'He's in a nasty mood.' 'Oh, don't fuss,' said the lady, 'he's only frightened. I can handle him. He quite likes me.'

This last remark so astonished Oliver that it took his breath away. Like that appalling woman! No sane cat, anywhere, would *ever* like the unspeakable Mrs Pike! She, meanwhile, supposing that Oliver had quietened because he felt friendly, boldly opened the cage door and put in her hand. 'Come on, Gospo, there's a good boy.' Oliver, without hesitation, grabbed her finger and bit hard. All the other cats burst into a cheer. 'Good old Oliver! Well done, kid!'

Mrs Pike screeched and slammed the cage door. 'Ee-eeh! He's bit me!' She waved her finger about; it was bleeding. 'Ungrateful beast! After all that coley and milk he's ate, too!'

'Be glad to see the back of this lot,' growled Wilberforce. 'Ain't half bin a load of Turks. Much more of this perishin' scratching and biting and you'll see me giving up cats altogether. Sooner tame lions, I would.'

'Sure, sure,' jeered Mrs Pike. 'You'd shine as a lion-tamer.'

'Shurrup!' bellowed Wilberforce, insulted by her tone. 'I don't blame that cat biting you; pity a few more don't bite you.'

'Don't you ask me to help you no more! Cage your own blooming cats!' shrieked Mrs Pike. And she scuttled from the room, leaving Wilberforce to get Oliver into the canary cage and the Guv'nor into Oliver's vacated cage single-handed. Wilberforce left the new cats in their baskets. 'It's only for the one night,' he muttered. 'All be hanging on clothes-racks in one of them groovy little boutiques soon.' And chuckling at the thought he switched off the light and went downstairs.

'Well,' said Nosher, once the cats found themselves on their own again, 'that was a bright thing to do, Guv. Come here to spring us and get nicked yourself.'

'Don't talk to me; just let me be, just let me be!' wailed the Guv'nor. 'Oh my head! My head!' And he curled himself up with his head in his paws, moaning.

'Got one of his migraines,' said Nosher. 'Trust him to get one at a time like this.'

'I don't think much of your mates if he's an example,' said Albert.

'Thought you was a gang of toughs,' said Selina.

'The good old Guv's tough enough,' said Nosher loyally 'Jus' accident prone.'

'Whatever the reason, the great rescue bid has failed,' said Binns, 'and we may as well face the fact that we're doomed. No use banking any longer on false hopes; we've had it.'

Faced with this terrible truth the cats were now beyond mewing or crying; beyond everything save total despair. In tortured silence they huddled in their cages and baskets. The long night ached itself away hour by hour, leaden with dread.

At last a pale, early morning light filtered through the window; the milkman was heard in the street; there were distant sounds of Mr and Mrs Pike moving about the house. Somebody opened the front door, shut it again. The wireless in the kitchen was turned on.

Presently the door of the prison-chamber was pushed open; the captives stirred and glanced up, quivering, expecting to see Wilberforce, come to put them in the van for their last journey. But instead of Wilberforce there walked into the room a young tabby cat with a strong bushy tail and very bright yellow eyes.

He glanced coolly about him and came to a stop by the cage of the Guv'nor, who was still curled up in a wretched ball, clasping his head, dead to the world. The newcomer stared at the Guv'nor for a moment or so, then shrugged and looked along the rows of the prisoners until he espied Nosher. He ran over to him, leapt lightly up on to the trestle, tested with his paw the fastening of Nosher's cage. 'Well old Nosh, they got you locked up proper,' he said.

'Cor, Scratch old fella, you don't know how good it is to see you!' gasped Nosher, hoarsely, barely able to speak with emotion. 'I always said you was the greatest . . .' His voice broke.

'Orright, orright,' said Scratch. 'Keep all that till later. Got to get you lot outa here.' He picked away with his claws at the catch on the cage door. 'How did the Guv get caught?'

'Oh, goofed it as usual. You know what he's like,' replied Nosher. 'And now, of course, he's got one of his migraines. Thank goodness you've turned up!'

'I guessed he musta got himself into some kinda trouble when he never come back after starting out to rescue you. I wanted to go with him in the first place, but the Guv swore he'd manage orright on his tod, and as I was on rat-duty until two o'clock this morning . . . There, that's got her!'

As he uttered these words Scratch flung open the door of Nosher's cage. Out Nosher sprang, rather stiffly. 'Blimey, my knees and ankles; talk about fixed!' he groaned.

'Never mind your knees and ankles, mush,' said Scratch.

27

'Let's get these other cats outa here before old what's-his-name comes up.'

Quickly and without wasting time in further talk Scratch and Nosher bounded from cage to cage, releasing their inmates. Scratch had to help Oliver down from the canary-cage; the poor young creature was so cramped he could hardly move. 'Try to jump about a bit more, loosen yourself up,' whispered Scratch. 'You got to run real fast in a minute.' The two cats who were taken from the baskets were equally stiff; they jerked their limbs and stared wildly round them, like animals in a nightmare.

The Guv, freed, clutched Scratch and mewed, 'Quick, quick, an asp'rin.'

'Don't be so flippin' daft; how should I have an aspirin?' snarled Scratch. 'Now listen, you lot; we're gonna creep downstairs; I'll open the front door, and we scarper, hard as we can. Once we're out in the street, it's each cat for himself. Dig?'

'But I don't know my way home!' wailed Sebastian.

The same dreadful thought had suddenly occurred to Oliver. 'Nor do I,' he faltered.

'Got no home to go to!' cried Selina.

'Then come with us, young 'uns,' snapped Scratch, impatiently. 'Only don't waste time yacking. We gotta move, and fast. Everyone else know their way home?'

The other cats mewed that they could take care of themselves. Scratch, without more ado, led the party, in single-file, downstairs. 'Keep well to the side; they creak in the middle,' he whispered. Oliver was still so stiff that he had to be partly supported by Nosher.

From the kitchen came the sound of the wireless; a weather-report. In the tiny, narrow hall hung a clock which ticked loudly and gloomily. 'Gimme a back,' said Scratch, advancing to the front door. Albert gamely took the stance of base. The abyssinian stood on his back, Nosher on him and Scratch then sprang on to Nosher's shoulders, balanced on his hind legs and, skilfully, with his forepaws, slid back the front door catch.

The door swung gently open with a tiny creak. 'Quick, run for it now!' hissed Scratch. The cats spilled into the mean, dirty street where the morning light was still thinly grey;

running swiftly and soundlessly they scattered in all directions and in a matter of seconds there was not one of them to be seen.

Oliver, unable to control his stiffened limbs, was borne away by Nosher and Scratch who each grasped him under a foreleg and whisked him along between them. Selina, Sebastian and the Guv'nor pattered speedily behind. Down one narrow street after another fled the cats; through muddy backyards, up murkey alley-ways; on and on; until Oliver was dizzy with the sensation of being rushed forward and ever forward.

At length the fleeing cats stopped for a breather behind a mountain of coke in a coal merchant's yard. They huddled in a silent little group, panting. Oliver glanced timidly at Nosher and Scratch, who still grasped him between them; Nosher, at close quarters, was certainly a tough-looking customer, while Scratch, although a decidedly young cat in years, was clearly equally old in experience, having a collection of scars of which a veteran warrior might have been proud, while his ears had been chewed nearly flat. Oliver felt almost as scared of these companions, although they had saved his life, as he had been of Wilberforce Pike. What had they in store for him, now that they had saved him? He, Oliver Simpkin, a young, beautifully brought up cat of excellent pedigree (his mother had been a Catterwaul before marriage, and as for the Simpkins, they dated back to King Felix the Fearless and had a family tree umpteen yards long), who had been warned time and time again never to play with rough cats in case he picked up fleas, bad language and coarse habits; who had been taught to be good and nice and polite and clean; who, in short, had been reared as a little gentleman, was henceforth to live in a Power Station with a gang of young tearaways.

But what choice had Oliver? The long flight across the enormous city had convinced the young cat that he was doomed to remain a homeless stray for the rest of his days; there were so many thousands of houses; so many, many families living in this vast landscape of bricks and cement, this never ending maze of streets and squares, that Oliver knew that he could never hope to find his own house and family again. Besides, thought poor Oliver, he would himself grow into a rough,

29

scruffy outcast like Scratch and Nosher, so that if he ever, by some miracle, found the Robinsons they would not even recognize him, let alone want him back as their pet.

At this point a voice was heard hailing them from a distance with a loud and breathless mew, 'Hey, there!'

The cats, surprised, looked round. A stout brindle figure was trotting across the yard.

'Why, it's that Albert!' said Selina. 'What does he want?' Sure enough, it was Albert. At last he reached them, much out of breath.

'Whew!' he said. '*Anno domini*, I fear,' The others stared at him blankly. 'Not so young as I was,' explained Albert. He paused, clearly a little embarrassed. Scratch said, 'What is it, mister? You changed your mind and wanna come with us?'

'Well, the truth is, I've always wanted to visit a Power Station,' confided Albert. 'You see, I've been in a police station, a railway station, a bus station and a fire station, being a school caretaker's cat and therefore in the habit of keeping well informed. And I thought, you know, that meeting you was too good a chance to miss of grasping the facts of the national grid. I shall only make a brief inspection, a quick look round, just to get the hang of the place.'

'Oh, orright,' said Scratch. 'Only we better ask the Guv'nor first.' He looked about him. 'Where's the Guv got to?' The Guv'nor was nowhere in sight.

'Oh, lor,' groaned Nosher, 'where's he landed himself now?'

The cats searched vainly in every direction. Then Nosher gave a whoop. 'There's his ears! But where's the rest of him?'

Sure enough, there were the Guv'nor's ears sticking out of a pile of coke. As the cats stared, the coke began to struggle and heave and then the Guv'nor sat up in the middle of it and started sneezing. 'You mighta pulled me out,' he said when at last he could speak. 'Trust you lot to leave a bloke to be buried alive.'

'Strike a light, Guv, we didn't even know you was there!' said Nosher.

'It beats me how you get yourself in these jams,' said Scratch, hauling the Guv'nor to his feet.

'I didn't get myself in anything,' retorted the Guv'nor peevishly. 'I was sitting listening to you lot talking when suddenly all this stuff came down on me, whoosh. I'm amazed that you never noticed.'

'Come to think of it,' said Nosher, 'I did hear a sort of rushing noise, but I didn't take no notice because I was too busy listenin' to Albert on about all the stations he's bin to.'

'Precisely,' said the Guv'nor. 'It's always the same. Everyone's far too busy to bother what happens to me.'

'Shouldn't have so many things happen to you, Guv,' said Scratch.

'If things keep happening that's not my fault,' said the Guv'nor. 'Happenings happen; fair enough, you can't expect happenings not to happen; but what I don't expect is always to find myself right in the middle of the happening when it happens. That isn't fair.'

'What's your sign?' asked Selina, sympathetically.

'What's my what?' snapped the Guv'nor, still very pettish.

'What star were you born under?' said Selina.

'How do I know? There are billions of stars; how am I to be expected to know which one was directly above me when I arrived?'

'Everyone has a star,' said Selina. 'I'm Aries.'

'You certainly are. A little too much for my fancy,' retorted the Guv'nor. 'You should get some trimmed off. You look like a gollywog.' And with that he turned round and stumped away.

'Coo!' said Selina. 'Sweet, ain't he?'

'He don't mean it,' said Scratch. 'Best natured cat in the world, really. Just that things tend to get on top of him.'

'Yeah, I noticed that,' said Selina.

Scratch and Nosher guffawed. 'Witty little kitten, isn't she?' said Nosher. 'Yeah,' replied Scratch, 'she's gonna brighten us up a lot.'

'Come on, let's get moving,' said Nosher.

Sebastian was still looking very weepy. Selina, noticing this, hooked a friendly little paw through his. 'Come on, Seb.' She gave him a motherly hug. 'You'll like the old Power Station ever so much when you get there. And we'll find your Miss What's-er-name for you in the end, won't we Scratch?'

'Sure thing,' said Scratch. 'Never say die.'

'Pringle,' whispered Sebastian. 'Miss P-Pringle.'

'We'll find Miss Pringle, come winter or springle, with crowds may she mingle, but we'll still find Miss Pringle,' said Nosher. Even Sebastian managed a small smile.

4. Oliver Takes an Oath

The second leg of the cats' journey to the Power Station was even longer than the first; a never-ending march, it seemed to the younger animals, who were weary indeed when at last, in the late afternoon, Scratch halted the party and pointed to three enormous chimneys rising above a vista of rooftops. From each chimney waved a giant plume of creamy smoke. 'There you are,' said Scratch. 'There she blows.'

'We gotta climb to the top of them chimbleys!' gasped Selina.

'Yeah,' grinned Nosher. 'That's where we live, up in the clouds.'

'Just the place for a nice little bird like you,' said Scratch.

He conducted them along the base of a strong green-painted metal fence which joined an enormously high brick wall that seemed to go on for ever. Set in this wall were equally enormous gates. Scratch drew up his party at these gates and the newcomers peered through them into a forecourt the size of a plain, full of parked cars and lorries. Across the yard was the largest building Oliver had ever seen; so huge that he boggled at its size. High, high above loomed the three chimney stacks and over all blew their smoke in a distant, swirling canopy.

'Here we are, folks,' grinned Nosher. 'Our little home.'

'We don't go in here,' explained Scratch, 'we got a private entrance.' He marched the cats back to the metal fence, between the bars of which they squeezed; they were now in a much smaller forecourt with a notice: *Office Staff Only*. There was a shrubbery, grass and flower beds. 'Mm, nice,' said Selina.

'This is the classy part. That's the superintendent's office over there,' said Nosher. The cats slipped through the shrubbery, crept under a dark archway, leapt a wall, landed among great mounds of coke, climbed another wall and filed along the top of it.

On the other side of the wall spread a public riverside walk with lawns and seats and trees. The river itself, very wide and shining, curved away, under bridges, into distances beyond imagination. The scene upon the opposite bank was of boat-yards, lighters, barges, moored craft of all kinds, shapes and sizes, a big house with a long green garden sloping down to the water, a party of ducks squatting on a little, lop-sided raft. Oliver stared at this scene, fascinated; all was entirely new to him.

Scratch now leapt down from the wall on to an enormous black pipe which snaked like a gleaming convex highway into a dark, throbbing labyrinth of pipes. The cats following him glimpsed shadowy shapes running out from between these pipes; for a horrifying instant Oliver feared that they might be giant rats, but then he saw that they were cats, gaily dancing out of their lairs in welcome.

At their head frisked the Guv'nor, now all smiles. 'So there you are at last!' he mewed. 'I hurried on ahead to tell the others you were coming. They've got us a smashing dinner!'

Nosher and Scratch were given a touchingly warm welcome by their cat comrades, who scampered round them slapping them on the back, pulling their ears and fondly roughing them up in general, to cries of, 'Good old Nosh! Good old Scratch! Thought you'd 'ad it that time, Nosh mate! Wotcha Scratch! Thought old Nosher worth rescuin' didja?'

The newcomers were then introduced. 'Three classy, no, two classy new mates for you. Selina 'ere, she's a rough 'un,' announced Nosher with his broadest grin. Selina uttered a pleased squeak but, acting outraged, swung her handbag hard at Nosher. Laughing, he fended it off with his paw. The other cats greeted this horseplay with delighted cheers. 'Young Oliver,' went on Nosher, now pulling Oliver forward, 'he's posh, but he's a good'un all the same; he bit old woman Pike's finger, he did. So give him a cheer for that, you lot!'

Everyone gave Oliver a cheer.

'And Sebastian here, well he ain't started biting yet, but he will all in good time,' said Nosher, kindly patting Sebastian, who hung his head and looked less like a biter than any

34

animal ever seen outside a toyshop. There were cheery shouts of, 'Bite 'em, kid!'

'And this fat old bloke,' went on Nosher, pointing to the highly indignant Albert, 'he wants to see round a Power Station.'

Everyone cheered Albert, but not, Oliver thought, in quite the way Albert really liked.

'Well,' said the Guv'nor, 'I'm sure you'll make four welcome new members of us Power Station lot. The more the merrier, I always say.'

'Thank you indeed,' said Albert, rather stiffly, 'but I am not going to stay. Just a quick look round, to get the hang of things.' He glanced at the jungle of pipes stretching in every direction. 'The national grid,' he said. 'The . . . er . . . harnessing of power.'

'There's a national grid over there, mister,' said one of the cats, very politely and with a very straight face.

'Where?' asked Albert, eagerly.

'There, see?' said a little marmalade girl cat with huge violet eyes. She pointed sweetly to a grating from which puffs of steam were rising. Albert, thanking her profusely, went across to look at it.

Oliver, Selina and Sebastian were jostled by the strange cats; Nibs, Boney, Twinkey, Sam, Crusoe, Randy and the little marmalade cat, Ninette. Sebastian clung tightly to Selina, who was not in the least shy and was soon chattering freely. Oliver found himself being asked about the incident of Mrs Pike's finger; he was too overwhelmed to say much.

Ninette and Selina eyed one another coldly. Selina said, 'Wot you done with your tail?'

'I'm a manx,' replied Ninette.

'You're a wot?'

'Manx cat.'

'Never 'eard of it,' grinned Selina.

'We're special cats; we don't have tails.'

'Poor old you,' said Selina. 'Thought you'd lost it.'

'Wouldn't give you tuppence for a tail.'

'Not for one like yours I wouldn't.'

'Them two have got their claws out,' grinned Nosher to Scratch.

'Old Ninette's bound to be jealous at first,' said the cat called Boney. 'Won't do her no harm to have another bird around. She's getting a bit stuck-up if you ask me, having no competition.'

At this point the Guv'nor decided that Albert should be shown over the Power Station before dinner. Albert, who had been staring very long and earnestly at the grating, was accordingly led away at the head of a party of cats, Twinkey and Sam remaining behind to finish cooking and serving the meal.

The Guv'nor acted as guide; he led Albert in and out amongst the pipes. The Guv'nor said, 'This is where we live; down here. You can see what a good place it is. We have this part mostly to ourselves; old Chalky and that lot don't come here much.'

'Who's old Chalky?'

'One of the humans who run this Power Station. There's quite a lot of them; they're very decent. Don't give us any trouble,' replied the Guv'nor.

'What are those pipes for?' asked Albert.

'Keep us warm,' replied the Guv, rather grandly.

The cats now ascended to the next floor; here stood a series of gigantic and mysterious machines which hummed and throbbed so loudly that Oliver couldn't hear himself think, let alone speak. Albert paraded slowly between these deafening monsters, looking learned. The Guv'nor then took the party up an iron staircase to inspect some more monsters and then down another staircase into a vast cavern. The roof of this cavern was so high that it could not be seen; a huge canopy of girders, aerial ladders and galleries, supported by steel pillars springing tree-wise from the floor, stretched overhead in a darkness from which flashed great yellow lamps, like tremendous stars. Oliver was reminded of an enormous rhododendron thicket that he had one night daringly explored; here was the same eerie, endless shadowy gloom, the same maze of twisted shapes high overhead, the same exciting lights in the dark vault of sky which soared, unfathomable, over all. For the first time in days he felt almost happy as he realized that the Power Station was going to be as thrilling a place to play in as the night-time garden of his old home had been.

Then he noticed that Sebastian was opening and shutting his mouth, trying to say something. Oliver leant towards him, expecting to hear some comment about the cavern. But Sebastian had other things on his mind. He was stammering, in a husky voice that was hard to hear, 'Miss Pringle said it was b-bad to b-bite.'

He looked shyly up at Oliver to see what Oliver's opinion was of this problem. Oliver replied, after a moment's hard thought, 'It depends on who you bite, I s'pose.'

'Yes,' said Sebastian, 'I sp-p-pose so.'

'Anyway,' said Oliver, after another pause for thought, 'I'm jolly glad I bit Mrs Pike.'

'I'm j-jolly g-glad too,' said Sebastian. And he giggled.

Meantime Albert, who was pretty clearly bowled over by the immensity of the Power Station but who was gamely determined not to show it, stood with his head tilted far back peering up at the girders, galleries and ladders. He twiddled round very slowly, three times, still peering upwards. 'Exactly,' he said. 'Precisely. It wouldn't work without 'em.' He resumed his normal posture and rubbed the back of his neck.

'Getting the hang of it, Albert?' asked Scratch.

'Oh, decidedly,' said Albert.

The Guv'nor led the party farther and farther into the cavern to where, in the centre, stood six black furnaces huge as mountains, towering upwards. From these came a strange sighing and throbbing and an aching, acrid smell, so that the cats shrank back, recognizing the sound and smell of great fire; that most fearful of all magics. In front of the furnaces slowly moved a belt of coke which was fed, steadily and endlessly, into their monster metal jaws, a horrific non-stop meal.

The cats huddled in a group at a respectful distance, staring. At last Albert, determined at all costs to keep his cool, took a few paces forward, gazed very hard at the vanishing coke, then stepped back again. 'Shedding the load,' he said. 'A simple case of shedding the load.'

The Guv'nor said, 'Orright. Now we'll show you something else.'

Albert was escorted to the rear of the furnaces. Here, in the

37

backside of one of them, was a small window, wide open. From this came a stream of intense heat and an eye-searing fire-glow. 'Now, just take a look in there, if you can,' said the Guv'nor.

The heat was so great and the glare so bright that to look for more than a moment was impossible, quite apart from the fact that the fire in itself was terrifying to the cats, driving them back while sheer curiosity dragged them forward. But one by one they did peer, fleetingly, through the little window, glimpsing another, enormous, country stretching magically in a dimension of its own for white-hot mile upon mile; a vast plain crossed by ranges of jagged red mountains, crumbling with heat, while thousands of little creatures frenziedly leapt and whirled in a dervish dance. Over all blew a blinding white wind in gusts and blasts, racing upwards and out of sight in a host of shining streamers.

'Oo, I don't like it!' said Selina. 'I can't look!' And she covered her eyes with one paw while clutching Scratch with the other. He put a paw round her to help her bear up. As for Albert, his eyes goggled, his jaw dropped and his whiskers trembled madly.

'Well?' the Guv'nor asked him.

'Ree-markable,' said Albert at last. 'Flummerghasting and totally stupendous. In short, somewhat baffling.'

The other cats exchanged meaning glances.

'I shall have to extend my stay for a few days, if you have no objection,' continued Albert. 'I will be frank and admit that it is going to take me a bit longer than I thought to get the hang of things here. What, at first sight, appeared a purely technical enterprise – men, machines and so forth, contains, I now see, a certain element of magic.'

'Stay as long as you like,' said the Guv'nor, pleasantly. To Nosher he murmured, 'Take him more than a day or two to get the hang of our Power Station.'

'Ask me, we got 'im 'ere for life,' whispered Nosher.

The cats now led Albert on an exploration in the cavern roof, amongst the girders and galleries. Here all was space and dizzy heights and the cats enjoyed themselves enormously, daring each other to creep along particularly narrow and breath-taking girders, to leap from ladders over terrifying drops, to race from gallery to gallery. Poor Albert, who was out of condition, kept stopping to inspect machinery. 'An interesting ding-bat, there,' he said to Oliver, casually, pointing to a confusing array of knobs and levers. Later, resting (Oliver suspected) at the top of a ladder, Albert explained, 'Just a moment's halt to cast an eye on these dimble-darts.' And he waved in the direction of a group of odd, bottle-shaped objects. Oliver, who knew nothing of machinery and cared less, merely said, 'Oh?' But he confided to Sebastian that he thought Albert was really less interested in ding-bats and dimble-darts than in snatching breathers.

After this, everyone felt that it was time for dinner. They returned to the basement where a wonderful spread awaited them. A great dish of rat-stew, 'Caught by old Nibs and Boney,' explained the Guv'nor, taking the role of master of ceremonies; a pile of sprats, 'Nicked from the market by Randy and Crusoe,' and an enormous veal and ham pie, 'Found by Ninette in a basket at the back of the George Hotel.' In addition there were enough bottles of catnip to keep everyone very happy for the rest of the evening.

Over dinner the cats who had been through the adventure with Wilberforce Pike talked spine-chillingly of capture, imprisonment and escape. The Guv'nor described how their cries for help had been heard by a prowling tom who had passed the news and the address of their prison-house along the cat-vine, until it had reached the Power Station cats and the Guv'nor had started out on his thrilling rescue mission; with catastrophic results. Scratch then took up the tale; how he had guessed that the Guv'nor must have been taken prisoner, too; how he had raced across the city to the Pike residence; how he had arrived there just as the newspaper boy had propped the morning paper behind the milk bottles on the front doorstep, whereat Scratch had hidden near the front door until Wilberforce had opened it to take in milk and paper; how, as the man scanned the front page of the paper, the cat had dodged into the house, to lurk behind an umbrella-stand while Wilberforce had taken the milk to the kitchen, leaving the coast clear for Scratch to dart upstairs and release the prisoners.

Each stage of this rescue story was greeted by cheers from the audience; when Scratch at last came to an end, the Guv'nor rose and drank his health and everyone joined in, following the toast with a fresh salvo of cheers, three times three. The health of all the rescued cats was then drunk, Boney proposing this toast. Then Nosher proposed a toast to 'Guv'nor Goofer' and that was drunk with cheers, and then the Guv'nor called for a toast to welcome Oliver, Sebastian and Selina, and so that was drunk, after which Nosher called for a toast to the health of Albert, and that was drunk. By this time Oliver, who had never before in all his life tasted anything stronger than a stolen swig of ginger-ale, felt himself becoming drowsier and drowsier, with the merry scene around him growing fuzzier and fuzzier and the faces of his fellow cats coming closer and closer to him and then fading farther and farther away again in a most peculiar and disconcerting fashion. Finally he saw a huge Guv'nor looming above him in a sort of mist and heard the Guv'nor's voice booming, 'And now I want everyone here, all you cats, on behalf of every cat in the kingdom, to take a solemn oath with me; a most solemn oath that you'll never go back on. All of us here heard tell of Wilberforce Pike, the cat thief, long before we met him.' (Loud boos and hisses.) 'We'd heard how no cat that got caught by Pike was ever seen again.' (Hisses.) 'But none of us really thought that we'd ever come up against this Pike. Well, all of us cats here now know all about old Pikey first hand.' (Great outbursts of catcalls, boos and hisses.) 'If good old Scratch hadn't come to our rescue like the great geezer he is, us lot that got caught would have had it. We'd all be fun-furs by now.' (Tremendous cheers of 'Good old Scratch!') 'Pr'aps we're the only cats that have ever escaped from Pike.' (Loud cheers.) 'So long as Pike's around there's not a single cat safe in this city. So long as that red-sprouter goes a-prowling round the streets of a night; him with his sack and his cat-basket and his nylon-fur tail what he 'tices pussies with; so long, I say, as that red-sprouter roams out of a night, there's not a cat nor a kitten can walk without fear and trembling.' (Loud, furious hisses, boos and cries of 'Shame!') 'So here's a solemn oath which I want you all to repeat after me: "I swear, by my whiskers and the full moon, that I shall never rest until Wilberforce Pike is caught and brought to justice." Now, together, swear it!'

The cats rose to their feet and shrieked the oath after the Guv'nor; Oliver heard himself spitting out the words with a force which made him feel a stranger to himself. Then the Guv'nor raised his glass and roared, 'And now fill up with catnip and drink this toast with me: HERE'S TO THE SPEEDY AND HORRIBLE END OF WILBERFORCE PIKE!'

The company filled their glasses and caterwauled in chorus 'TO THE SPEEDY AND HORRIBLE END OF WILBERFORCE PIKE!' After which there was a lot more drinking and much singing, but about this Oliver knew nothing, for the words of the toast were no sooner out of his mouth than his tumbler slipped from his paw and he flopped behind a nice warm pipe into a bottomless well of sleep.

5. The Great Banquet Robbery

When Oliver woke next morning, dazedly, to find himself lying in a cobwebby corner beneath a huge iron pipe, he was unable at first to think where he could be. Close at hand a funny little voice was singing:

> Roses are red, kitten,
> Vi'lets are blue,
> Sugar is sweet, kitten,
> An' so are you . . .

Oliver stood up, stretching himself, and peered forth. There sat Selina with a minute piece of mirror propped in front of her, singing to herself and doing her hair. Oliver now remembered where he was.

'Hello, you woke up at last?' said Selina, noticing him. 'Thought you was gonna lie there all day.'

'Where is everyone?' asked Oliver.

'Dunno. Tell the truth I haven't been up so long myself. That was a smashin' party last night, wasn't it?'

Oliver could in fact remember very little of the party, but he agreed that it had been a good one.

'You glad you come here?' went on Selina. 'I am; ever so. All that talk about giant-rats an' that, old Nosher was just trying to take the micky, if you ask me. I think it's smashing here; I reely do.' And she started singing and doing her hair again.

Sebastian and Albert appeared, both looking cheerful. 'C-come and p-play outside,' said Sebastian. 'It's nice.'

'Extraordinarily pleasant,' agreed Albert.

'Orright,' said Selina. 'Just gimme a jiffy to powder me nose.'

'A wash,' said Albert, severely, 'is what some of us need.'

'I beg your pardon?' said Selina, huffily.

'Prinking and powdering and puffing out one's hair,' said Albert, 'won't help much when one is . . . er . . . mm . . . basically dusty, as it were.'

'Dusty yerself!' snapped Selina. And, gathering up her powder-compact and handbag, she flounced off, much miffed.

'The young of today,' said Albert, 'have never been taught that a good wash, every morning, is a cat's first duty. *First duty!*' He stared hard at Sebastian and Oliver, neither of whom had washed, to tell the truth, since their capture by Wilberforce. 'I have washed,' said Albert, smugly. 'Others may have done so too; on the other hand, they may not. I make no comment mark you; but a good wash is a good wash, and it shows. As does its absence. I repeat, I make no comment. Washing is a matter of morale. Give me a cat who washes regularly and *properly*, not a mere matter of a lick and a promise . . . Give me such a cat and I will say, without a moment's hesitation, "Sir," I will say, "sir, that cat there . . ." '

'Let's b-buzz off,' whispered Sebastian to Oliver. The two young cats stole away. Behind them Albert's voice dwindled, ' ". . . is an animal with whom I would go into the jungle" . . .'

In the riverside gardens the autumn sunshine was bright and a small wind sent droves of leaves running over the ground. The cats walked through a shrubbery and paused at its edge; Sebastian was wearing a pensive expression, which Oliver was beginning to think of as his 'Pringle look'. Sure enough, Sebastian said, at last, 'Miss P-Pringle said always t-to wash, too.'

'So did Mrs Robinson.'

There was a thoughtful pause.

'If we get too dirty, and then meet them again, our families, I mean, they mightn't want us back,' observed Oliver.

Without more ado the two young animals found a retired, sunny spot behind a shed and washed themselves thoroughly. It took a while. When at length they had finished they amused themselves with a merry game of chasing leaves. In the middle of this the cat named Crusoe appeared, obviously excited.

'Come on, you two, there's a raid!'

'Raid! Where?' asked Oliver.

'At the Guildhall. Where's the others?' And Crusoe scurried off to collect Albert and Selina.

'What's a G-Guildhall?' inquired Sebastian.

'Don't know,' said Oliver, 'but we'll find out.'

Soon he, Sebastian, Albert and Selina were racing after Crusoe along riverside wharves and alley-ways. Selina, as usual, was agog with questions.

'Where we goin'?''

'Like I said, Guildhall,' said Crusoe.

'Whassat?'

'Where the Mayor hangs out.'

'Who's 'e?'

'Old geezer with a yeller chain round his neck.'

'Wot's he want a chain for?'

'Search me.'

'What we goin' there for?'

'Knock off the ole Mayor's banquet.'

'Whatsa banquet?'

'Biggest feast in history. All spread out, ready, and Nosher's founda winder we can climb in and nick it all,' panted Crusoe.

'Is there chicking?' asked Selina, her eyes very round and bright.

'Chicking, and a whacking great lumpa salmon, and a huge ham, and cream cakes . . .' Crusoe had no breath left for more.

'Cool' exclaimed Selina, in ecstasy, 'I can't wait!'

The Guildhall proved to be a very large building with a striped awning over the steps. 'They always put that up when there's gonna be a Mayor's do. That's how we can tell,' explained Crusoe. 'Other times we never bin able to get in, so we go round the dustbins arterwards and even then we get smashin' stuff, but this time, while ole Nosher was casing the joint, he spotted this winder open and climbed up an' looked in and he says it's the biggest bloomin' spread you ever set eyes on. Come on, this way; careful, we don't want anyone to see us.'

The cats slunk through a yard at the rear of the Guildhall; it was full of boxes, bins, hampers and crates, between which the animals dodged skilfully. In a corner of the yard, behind some large packing-cases, they found the Guv'nor holding a council of war.

'The whole point of this job,' the Guv'nor was explaining,

'is that it can't be done in bits. I mean we can't do it like one cat climbs in and nicks a pie for himself, and then after a bit another gets in and swipes some salmon, and so on. There's a lot of old women keeps dancin' about, fussing over this and that; if they spot a cat anywhere near that grub they'll shut that window and we'll have had it. So this job's got to be carefully planned.'

'Are we gonna eat it on the spot?' asked Nosher. Scratch said, 'How can we, with all them old women around? They'll come in and catch us. We'll have to scarper with the stuff and eat it afterwards.'

'That's the ticket,' said the Guv'nor. 'Lift the stuff and whip off with it quick to some nice quiet place where we can scoff the lot in peace.'

'Do we all go in together, then?' asked Boney.

'Yeah,' said the Guv'nor. 'All go in together; if we do get spotted there'll be so many of us all running in different directions that they'll never catch a single one of us.'

'We better open some of the other windows,' suggested Nibs. 'Then if we do have to run for it we shan't be all queuing up to jump out the same window.'

'Good idea,' said the Guv. 'How about it, Scratch? You're our prize cracksman.'

Scratch agreed to try to open some of the other windows and soon stole off on this errand; meanwhile, the Guv'nor continued to organize the raid. 'We must have this job planned to the last detail,' he kept repeating. 'The last detail. Everyone must know what they've got to do, and do it like clockwork.'

'How we gonna pinch the grub; each take what we fancy?' said Boney.

'No; lead to chaos, that would,' replied the Guv'nor. 'We must have it all worked out in advance who takes what.'

'Vote I takes the chicking!' shrilled Selina. Boney retorted, 'You won't get nothing if you go on like that!'

'First step is to ask old Nosher to tell us exactly what he saw and then we can organize who runs off with which,' said the Guv'nor.

'Give us a list of what you seen, Nosh,' said Twinkey.

Nosher replied, 'Biggest bloomin' spread, mate, that I ever set eyes on, or my name ain't Nosher.'

'Yeah, mate, but itemize, itemize,' said Crusoe.

'Item what?'

'Name the things.'

'There was a great big ham, and a whacking big salmon, and a huge great cream cake, like a wheel; straight, no kidding, the size of a lorry wheel.'

'Whew!' said all the cats.

'And salads galore; you know, lobster, chicken, sorta mixed up in big dishes . . .'

'Very delicious, but we can't carry them,' said the Guv'nor. 'It's the ham, the salmon and the giant cream cake we shall need to concentrate on. What else d'you see?'

'Round brown things. Smallish.'

'Hm; sound like rissoles to me. They'll be easy to carry. How near to the windows is all this grub?'

'The tables are right under the winders; it's dead easy. All you got to do, Guv, is jump from the window-sill, right down amongst the food. Can't go wrong with that one. Problem will be cathandling the ham and the cake; them big things.'

'Divide ourselves into teams,' said the Guv'nor. 'So many cats for the cake, so many for the ham, and so on; bob's your uncle.'

Scratch returned in due course; he had contrived to open two extra windows. 'But we better get on with the job pronto, Guv, before some interferin' geezer comes along an' shuts 'em all up again.'

Quickly it was decided that the burliest cats, Scratch, Nosher, Nibs and Randy should steal the ham; that Twinkey, Sam and Albert should cope with the salmon and, that the Guv'nor, Boney and Crusoe should cathandle the monster cream cake. Ninette, Selina, Sebastian and Oliver were each to take as many smaller items, such as pies, patties and rissoles, as they could manage. The ham team was to have one window, the salmon team another, while the cream cake team was to share a window with the girl cats and Oliver and Sebastian.

The Guv'nor lined up his troops in battle order: ham team, salmon team, cream cake team and what he called 'The

Snatch-and-Grab Kids'. Stealthily he led the four teams to crouch under the windows; one window had been closed, leaving only two open. This hitch in his plans made the Guv'nor chitter with rage. 'Meddlesome humans. Always sticking their long noses . . .'

'The busy-body biped is a by-word of botheration,' said Albert, in his school-master voice. The Guv'nor snapped, 'Look, mister, I've no time for tongue-twisters and party games now!'

'I assure you, I had no intention . . .' began Albert. Scratch said, 'Not to worry, mate. Ham and fish go in at that window on the left, cake and Snatch-and-Grabbers on the right. How's that, Guv?'

'Have to do,' replied the Guv'nor. He raised his voice: 'Ready, you lot? I shall start a count-down of ten, and when I say ONE then you all run to your window. And the best of feline luck,' He then began counting, 'Ten, nine, eight . . .'

It seemed to Oliver that ONE was an eternity away; but then the Guv'nor was hissing, 'One!' and all the cats were galloping like mad towards the building.

The windows were first-floor, quite high from the ground. The ham and fish parties sprang in rapid succession on to the sill of their window and vanished through it, although the portly Albert, who went last, had rather a job to heave himself up. The cream cake party, led by the Guv'nor, charged their window, through which the Guv'nor soared in jet style, not bothering to alight on the sill. There was no time for the cats coming behind to admire this athletic display; they were too engrossed themselves in running and springing for the sill. It was a big leap for a young cat, and Oliver landed on the sill much out of breath, to find that the cats of the cream cake party who should all have been down on the table by now, grappling with the cake, were, with the exception of the Guv'nor, still huddled on the sill, staring downwards in wild horror. Oliver too craned forward to look; there, immediately below, was a vast cream cake, exploded into fragments; cream, chocolate, fluffy sponge, walnuts and candied cherries were spread in all directions, while from the centre of this horrible gooey mess protruded the frantically kicking hind legs and waving tail of the luckless Guv'nor Goofer.

It was clear that his Nijinski-like bound through the window had carried him to his target with an excess of gusto: he had scored a bull's-eye, head-first. But again, events were crowding too fast for thought; Oliver peered, in a flash guessed what had happened, muttered, 'Whew!' and then Sebastian, Selina and Ninette landed together behind him on the little that was left of the overcrowded sill. To keep themselves from toppling backwards they flung themselves forward; the mass of cats overbalanced and hurtled, head-first in their turn, in the wake of the Guv'nor. Most of them landed on top of him, or alongside him, in the smashed cream cake, but Oliver and Sebastian plunged into a huge bowl of mixed fruit-salad and floundered there in danger of drowning amongst sliced peaches, pears, pineapple, grapes and apricots.

They were still struggling to clamber out when Oliver heard that high-pitched, female shrieking which always spelt trouble. The cats had been discovered! The shrieks grew louder; Oliver sensed, rather than saw, large women bearing down upon him. Desperately he managed to heave himself out of the fruit-salad bowl and hauled Sebastian after him. Together they sprang for the window and, an instant later, were racing back to the Power Station.

Safely there they crouched by a warm pipe and washed themselves all over again; they felt horribly sticky and found that they tasted of pineapple.

'What do you sup-p-pose has happened to the others?'

'Dunno. I hope that the old Mayor won't eat 'em.'

'Miss P-Pringle always said not to steal.'

At that moment Ninette and Selina came staggering in, each weighed down with rissoles. Although gasping for breath, they were clearly very pleased with themselves.

'Look wot I got!' panted Selina. 'Chicking what-d'you-call-'ems!' She began arranging her booty on the floor, as if setting out a game of patience. 'See how many I got! All them ole women, screechin' their heads off; but they didn't stop me getting my chicking!' She waggled her head delightedly. Oliver noticed that she had cream in her hair.

'I got more than you,' said Ninette.

'Oh no you ain't, ducky.'

Three more cream-clotted cats now came lurching in, supporting a shapeless white figure shambling blind, like a zombie. At this gruesome apparition the four young cats stared in horror. The zombie attempted to speak, but simply made thick, strange, clotted sounds. He pawed about him; feeling to find out where he was. It dawned upon the gaping Oliver that this ghostly creature was the Guv'nor soused in cream; eyes, ears, nose and mouth plugged with cream.

His companions were in not much better shape, but at least they could see and speak. They propped the Guv'nor against a pipe.

'We shall have to lick him clean,' said Boney.

'I can't, mate,' said Crusoe. 'I've swallered so much cream meself that to lick any more off 'im will make me sick.'

'Well, scrape off the top layer, then start licking.'

'Get them young 'uns to do it; I've had enough blooming cream to last me a lifetime.'

'You lot find some little sticks to scrape the Guv'nor down,' said Boney, turning to the young animals. They ran into the gardens and returned with suitable twigs; the Guv'nor had now managed to clear his throat of cream and was talking to Boney in a peculiar, oily sort of half-voice. Crusoe had disappeared.

'Found myself zooming slap bang into it,' the Guv'nor was saying. 'Felt it explode all round me, squish! Talk about creamy smotherings!'

'Forget it, Guv, forget it,' said Boney, who did not look very well.

'Delicious,' said the Guv'nor. 'Golopshous, in fact. But after a bit I must say I did start to feel . . .'

'Talk about something else, shall we?'

The young cats squatted round the Guv'nor in a circle, scraping the cream off him. He said, 'I hope you've got a dish.'

'D-dish?' queried Sebastian.

'Yes, to put the cream in. We don't want to waste it.'

Boney rushed out.

'He gone to fetch one?' asked Selina, staring after him.

'I don't think so,' said Oliver.

49

In the middle of this scraping session Albert, Twinkey and Sam returned with a sizeable booty of salmon. Albert had had a chair thrown at him by a human and as a result was limping rather badly. The salmon party exclaimed over the Guv'nor, saying what jolly rotten luck it was that he had landed in the cake, the Guv'nor and the other cats exclaimed over the salmon, saying how jolly good to have carried off such a super lot of it with all those old women screaming and throwing things! In the midst of all this talk there was a rolling, rattling sound as of small metal wheels, and Nosher, Scratch, Nibs and Randy arrived; dragging along the ham which was strapped on to a roller-skate, as if on a trolley. This brainwave of a notion, they explained, had come from Scratch who, as they had staggered up an alleyway, half dead with the weight of the ham and expecting to be arrested any moment, had noticed a small boy learning to skate, using only one skate while the other lay on the ground a few yards distant. To run off with the skate had been the work of a trice, and in an empty garage the four cats had lashed the ham to their improvised truck. After which the journey home had been easy.

All in all, therefore, the gang felt that their raid might be judged a success. They had got away with a huge ham, a large quantity of salmon and several chicken rissoles. There was also a dish of cream scraped from off the Guv'nor. The only major casualty had been the giant cream cake itself. 'You bombed into that one, Guv, like you was a real block-buster,' chuckled Nibs.

'Talk about a squelch!' said the Guv'nor.

'Good job it did go squelch, Guv,' said Nosher. 'If it had bin a Dundee cake, or something solid, you'd've gone squelch yourself, you would.'

The food was set out in a secluded place among the pipes and there left for a while, since everyone had a certain number of chores and duties to perform before dining.

Oliver, Sebastian, Selina and Twinkey took turns helping the Guv'nor to lick himself clean. Ninette applied cream to Albert's bruised hock (where the chair had struck him) and then put a bandage round it for support. Scratch and the ham-gang took the roller-skate back to the alley so that the small boy might find it. 'Only a heel steals from kids,' said Scratch. Sam was dispatched to what the Guv'nor grandly called 'the cellar' to fetch up bottles of catnip.

At last it was time for the feast. With the Guv'nor at their head the cats trooped, tails up, purring with pleasure, to the cosy spot under the pipes where the ham, salmon, rissoles and cream had been so carefully set out.

But when the cats got there, not a trace of food remained! 'Massacred mice!' bawled the Guv'nor, beside himself. 'The grub's all gone! It's been stolen!' He rolled furious, glaring green eyes round the empty lair; there was a trail across the dusty floor where somebody, or something, had dragged the ham and all round the ham-trail were dirty footprints. Scratch bent to examine them briefly, then looked up with a grim expression.

'Rats,' he said.

'Rats!' roared the Guv'nor. 'Dirty thieves! Rotten robbers! Orright, they've asked for it this time! Come on you lot! We'll give 'em rats!'

And snarling furiously he pounded off along the ham-trail, with all the other cats, spitting vengeance, pressing behind.

6. The General Loses a Tail

The ham-trail led through a maze of pipes to a hole in a wall. An attempt had been made by the rats to get the ham through this hole; there were smears of fat all round it. Clearly, the rats had found the ham too large to go in and so they had dragged it instead through a doorway, across a yard and down a much larger hole behind a vast coal-bunker.

The angry cats gathered at the mouth of the large hole; the Guv'nor said, 'I'm going in. Who's coming with me?'

Everyone chorused that they were.

'Mind you, it may be very nasty down there,' warned the Guv'nor.

'It *will* be very nasty down there,' said Scratch. 'That's where I got my ears chewed pretty well off. If the General comes out fighting you meet him head-on, down there in a tunnel, like, and it's too narrer to turn round; you can take my word for it, you'll find it very rough while it lasts!'

'All the same, I'm going in,' said the Guv'nor.

Everyone else chorused that they were going in too.

So in went the Guv'nor without more ado and one by one all the other cats followed.

Scratch, Boney and Nosher went in on the tail of the Guv'nor; Ninette, who was a first-rate fighter, went in behind Nosher. Then came the other cats. Sebastian, Oliver and Selina were ordered in last. Selina did not at all like the feeling of being the very last, she had a nasty fear that something would creep up behind her, so Oliver took her place.

The hole led, as Scratch had said, into a dark and narrow tunnel, along which the cats crawled and squeezed with considerable difficulty. They had not gone far before the Guv'nor stopped short; whereat there was a pile-up of cats. The Guv'nor hissed, as well as he could, over his shoulder to Scratch, 'Where do we find ourselves at the end of this?'

'I dunno,' hissed back Scratch. 'Only time I ever bin down here the General come out and met me, fighting, long before I got to the end.'

The Guv'nor resumed his advance along the tunnel. Everyone else crowded forward accordingly.

Suddenly the Guv'nor stopped again. 'Whassat?'

'Wot's wot?' gasped Scratch, his mouth full of the Guv'nor's tail.

'Thought I saw something moving,' whispered the Guv.

'You can't miss the General when he comes,' said Scratch. 'You see his little red eye. You know it's him, 'cos he's only got the one.'

The Guv'nor shuddered slightly, then began crawling forward again; the queue of cats behind him likewise. But after a couple more yards or so he halted once more. 'O-o-ooh!'

'What?' hissed Scratch.

'Can't you see it?'

'Can't see nothing except your bottom,' snapped Scratch. All this stopping and starting was getting on his nerves.

'Red eye; I saw it flash!'

'Then grit yer teeth, mate, for he's comin'.'

The Guv'nor stiffened, Scratch stiffened; every cat felt the cat ahead of him stiffen and so stiffened likewise.

'Well?' growled Scratch, after several very long-seeming seconds, during which he had stood bracing himself to meet the General's charge.

'I . . . I think I must've imagined it,' murmured the Guv'nor, apologetically.

He resumed his creeping forward. The young cats at the end of the queue, finding themselves on the move again, exchanged amused remarks. 'Here we g-go,' said Sebastian. 'Real f-frenzied advance, isn't it?'

'Mind your tail, Seb. I don't wanta eat it,' said Selina. 'Blimey, this tunnel's getting tighter and tighter!'

'It's a wonder they got that ham along here,' said Oliver.

Suddenly they found themselves again bumping one against the other.

'Ouch!' said Sebastian.

'Oh lor!' gasped Selina. 'Don't mind me!'

'What's biting them up in front?' asked Oliver.

The Guv'nor and Scratch were involved in fresh and heated argument.

'Jumping jimps; my head!' wailed the Guv'nor.

'Stone it, you can't get one of your flaming migraines now, Guv! Get a move on, do!'

'We'll have to turn round and go back!' said the Guv'nor.

'Turn round? You flaming daft? How can we turn round? There's no room.'

'We'll *have* to turn round. I've just bumped my head on the end of the tunnel!'

'Tunnel doesn't just end like that. It can't.'

'It does. I just knocked my head on it.'

'Rats!'

'Where?' gasped the Guv.

'Holy Joe Soakes! Talk about a nutter!' sighed Scratch. Aloud he said, 'For rats, read rot. Rot that you hit your head on the end of the tunnel.'

'But I did. I'm slap bang up against . . . I tell you, it's solid rock.' There was a pause. Then the Guv'nor said, 'No it's not. It's ham.'

'It's *what*?'

'Ham.'

'Come off it.'

'But it is. I've just ate a bit.' There was another pause. 'Dee-licious!' sighed the Guv'nor.

'They must've got the old ham stuck in the tunnel!'

'Mm . . . mm . . . mmm.'

'Then we'll have to go back. And we can't turn round, so we'll all have to go back backwards.'

'Mm . . . mm . . . mmm. Cooked to a T.'

Scratch hissed to Boney behind him, 'Back out. Tunnel's blocked. Pass it along.'

The message travelled along the tunnel. At last it reached the end of the queue. Sebastian said, 'Hey, Selina! Oliver! Albert's too stout. T-tunnel's blocked. We're to g-give him a song!'

'Poor old Albert!' gurgled Selina. And she began to sing,

'Roll Out the Barrel'. The other cats near her joined in. By degrees the song travelled up the queue until it reached the distracted Scratch and Guv'nor.

Oliver was in the midst of song when suddenly he felt, rather than heard, a rush of feet behind him.

Kitten-lissom and inspired with such an acute sense of danger that he could do things that normally he could not have done, the young cat doubled himself into a ball and whipped round in the narrow tunnel, stem to stern, just in time to glimpse a small spot of fire flashing up and down and drawing closer and closer. There was a suffocating, musky, musty smell. A vast humped black body bounding crookedly, with an evil half-slewed gait, hurtled hard at him. Huge yellow fangs flashed; Oliver shot out his claws and slashed. Then there was a chaos of squealing, yowling, biting, chopping, clawing; hisses, shrieks, violent flickers and jabs of pain, that he felt without truly being aware, fury and hatred, murderous moments of flying fur and a salty taste of blood in his mouth: a battle to the death.

An irresistible force from behind him drove Oliver along the tunnel through a storm of violence; he fought blindly, instinctively, and went on fighting. He was interlocked with a kicking, writhing, fang-gnashing monster. He felt one of his ears go and swore with pain and fury; he bit and cuffed and tore. Then what felt like a whip began flailing his face; Oliver snapped, clamped his teeth into something and set them hard. There was a high-pitched, non-stop shrieking. At that moment too there was daylight, white and dazzling, and a seething blackness of rats all running from him, and then an avalanche of cats spilling and somersaulting and hurling themselves after the rats. Oliver stood stock still; utterly out of breath. Then the cats were racing back, cheering and dancing round him. He found, to his amazement, that he had an enormous rat-tail gripped between his teeth; a tail dirty, bare and pink, sprouting a few black hairs from its nakedness, and tied at the tip with a grubby red satin bow.

Sebastian, all eyes, was gaping at it. 'What's that?'

'It's the General's tail!' bawled Nosher. 'Old Oliver's got the General's tail, red ribbon and all!'

The rejoicing which followed bewildered Oliver even more than the fighting had done. He was paw-shaken, back-slapped and hugged by all the other cats, who told him how jolly well he had fought, standing up to the General face-to-face, driving him backwards out of the tunnel by sheer ferocity and fighting-skill; finally putting the General and his whole army to flight by the seizure of the General's tail. In short, Oliver had covered himself with glory. Selina and Sebastian had distinguished themselves, too, by the brave way in which they had done everything they could to support Oliver.

'Do us great credit, you kids do, great credit,' said the Guv'nor. 'We're dead chuffed to have you in our gang, and that's a fact.'

The cats all trooped back to their lair among the pipes, Oliver walking at their head, carrying the General's tail. Sebastian and Selina walked either side of him. All the other cats sang, 'When the saints come marching in'. Once in the lair the tail was nailed to the wall and Oliver sat in the place of honour under it. A great session of catnip and song was held; unfortunately there was nothing to eat, but everyone was too happy drinking Oliver's health and Selina's health and Sebastian's health and singing and caterwauling to be very much troubled by the lack of victuals. Every now and again one cat would ask another, 'I wonder how the old General feels without his tail?' And then there would be a great guffaw of laughter and another song.

General Squeals and his chief aide-de-camp, Sergeant Fleaby, were holding a council of war in the General's bunk-house; a squalid cellar-apartment, deep under the river bank, to which the General always retired when he felt himself in any particular danger.

They were an evil-looking pair: sooty-furred, hump-shouldered, all fangs and claws, bristling whiskers and glitter-ing eyes. The General, in addition to the famous black patch, now wore a bloodstained bandage round his head and another round the stump that was all that remained of his tail. This wound made sitting-down painful for him, so he stood propped against a battered old chest-of-drawers crammed with rags

56

papers, half-chewed candle-ends and gnawed bones. The Sergeant was seated at a rickety wooden table on which stood a bottle; this the two rats passed to one another, turn and turn about.

At last the General spoke: 'That was a smashin' tail I 'ad there, Sergeant; a real stunner. You won't never set eyes on a tail like that again, not if you lives to be a 'undred.'

'Longest tail I ever see, sir, that was. And I tell no lie,' said Sergeant Fleaby loyally.

'Faberlous tail it were, faberlous,' said the General. 'And not only long, thick too. No kiddin', Fleaby; at the top end it were nigh on a hinch thick.'

'More like hinch-anderarf, sir.'

'Best bloomin' tail any rat ever 'ad,' sighed the General. 'Gimme that bottle, Serg.'

'Bottle comin' up, sir,' said Fleaby.

The General took the bottle, put it to his lips, shut his eye, gave a long long pull, wiped his mouth and opened his eye, shook his head, sighed again and handed the bottle back to the Sergeant.

'And now them cats is a-eatin' it,' said the General. 'A-scrunchin' it up, they are, like a prime juicy bitta bacon-rind. I can see it in me mind's eye, Fleaby. I can 'ear 'em a-scrunchin' in my himagines.'

'I 'ope it disagrees with 'em; 'ope it gives 'em gyp, I do, sir.'

'I tell you, Fleaby, I'd part with my other eye to get even with them cats, straight I would.'

'Pity they ever got away from old Wilberforce, sir.'

'It were an' all.' There was a long and moody silence, during which the rats each took another pull at the bottle.

'Our lads didn't show fight today, Fleaby. Miserable yeller-bellied lot they was today. Fair enough, I 'ad to lead the advance; fair enough I caught the worse of it up that tunnel, but when all the cats come tumblin' out into the open, well, then I expected our lads to show their teeth; but, blimey, all they showed was their tails!'

''Cos they seed your's, red bow an' all, sir, danglin' between that young cat's teeth, sir. Demoralizin', that was, sir; dee-moralizin'.'

'Wish I could think of some way of dee-moralizin' them cats.'

There was another pause; more swigs.

'Wish I could get that Wilberforce Pike along 'ere,' mused the General. 'Tip 'im a wink; there's cats galore down 'ere. He'd soon settle that lot.'

There was another long pause.

'If I 'ad a bitta paper I could write 'im a letter,' said the General.

'If you could write,' grinned Fleaby.

The General whipped into an instant fury. 'Wot you mean, if I could write? Course I can write! Cor, strike it! Oughter be shot, I ought, if I can't write. Lived along of 'umans long enough, I 'ave, to be able to write, and so ought you be able.'

Sergeant Fleaby looked abashed.

'Gimme a bitta paper,' snapped the General.

'Yessir.'

'An' a . . . somethink to write with.'

The Sergeant scrummaged about in the chest-of-drawers and finally produced a half-torn page of an old exercise book and a small piece of pencil. The General seated himself, very uneasily, at the table, licked the pencil and fell into deep thought. He sat frowning and staring at the paper while the expectant Sergeant breathed heavily down his neck.

'Lemme see,' muttered the General. 'Lotta cats. Bagsa cats. 'Undreds of cats . . .' He sucked hard at the pencil, then poised it ready for action. The excited Sergeant gasped, 'You gonna write it in wiggle, sir?'

'No. Old Pike's too higorant for wiggle. Gotta be basic ABC for Pikey.'

And the General wrote, licking his pencil every other letter:

LOOK OWT PIK.

Then he stopped. 'Gimme that bottle.'

The Sergeant thrust the bottle on to the table in front of the General who took a very long drink indeed. Then he wrote some more:

Then he stared at what he had written.

'Wot's it read, sir?' asked the Sergeant at last, unable to bear the suspense any longer.

'Look out Pike; there's bags of cats at the Power Station,' declaimed the General.

'Cor!' Fleaby shook his head in wonderment and admiration. 'That'll work the trick, sir.'

'It should,' said the General, much pleased with himself.

'Want me to run it round to old Pike's 'ome, sir?'

'No, I'll take it meself. A walk won't do me no 'arm. Don't want me wounds to get stiff.' And after another session with the bottle the General folded his letter, tucked it inside the band round his head, perched on top of the bandage a battered old cocked-hat trimmed with dirty gold lace, strapped on a holster with one small, but very ugly-looking pistol and, thus equipped, loped lopsidedly away.

He made the journey mainly underground, through sewers. At last, reaching the neighbourhood of his destination, he took to rat-runs, finally squeezing out of a hole in a brush-and-broom cupboard in the Pike's kitchen. The General gently opened the cupboard door a crack; not a human in sight! He ran across the floor, leapt on to a chair and from thence on to the table; here he enjoyed a quick snack of half a cold sausage that he found stuck to a plate. He placed his letter beside the plate, sprang down from the table and was scuttling back to the cupboard when Mrs Pike entered, glimpsed him and screamed.

Later she told Wilberforce, 'A huge great rat, the size of a cat, wearing a cocked-hat and a black patch over one eye and a bandage round his tail: clear as I'm seein' you.'

'Sure he warn't pink?' jeered Wilberforce.

But the letter on the table was something that Wilberforce couldn't dismiss. 'Someone musta dropped it in while you popped round to the baker's,' said he to Mrs Pike, who merely replied that whoever it was that left the letter they ought to be ashamed at not being able to write and spell better than *that*.

'Nemmind the spelling and writing, it's the message wot counts,' said Wilberforce. 'Bags of cats is wot it says; bags of cats at the Power Station, it looks like. And bags is wot we wants, my love. So hang the spelling and writing.'

7. Front Page Story

The Guv'nor expected reprisals from the General and his horrid rat legions: the cats were convinced that he would try to recapture his tail. So they mounted guard over it night and day, two cats at a time, each taking a turn.

One afternoon, when Oliver and Sebastian were on guard duty, stationed one each side of the celebrated tail, and so bored that they were playing 'I Spy with My Little Eye', a stranger appeared.

Sebastian said, 'I sp-p-py with my little eye s-s-something b-beginning with essss . . .'

'Esss?'

'Y-yesss.'

'Sparrow?'

'No.'

'Spider?'

'No.'

'Soot?'

'No.'

'I give up.'

'No, g-go on.'

'Oh well . . . er . . . sealyham.'

'No. Anyway, I c-can't see one.'

'Selina?'

'No.'

'Scoop!' said a loud voice.

Oliver and Sebastian whipped round to stare in the direction of the voice. They found themselves looking at a very large, muscular, indeed in all ways tough manx cat; long-legged, lop-eared, green-eyed. This redoubtable animal surveyed Oliver and Sebastian with a broad and not unkindly grin. '*Saludos*,' he said. 'What goes on here?'

'We're playing "I Spy With My Little Eye",' explained Oliver, rather lamely. 'And we're on guard,' he added.

'Oh? Guarding what?'

'The General's tail,' said Oliver, nodding towards that un-beautiful trophy.

'He b-b-bit it off!' said Sebastian.

'Who bit it off what?' replied the stranger.

'Oliver b-bit it off the General,' said Sebastian.

'Did he, by Jupiter!' said the stranger. 'Some tail, that!'

'It's true!' flashed Sebastian, very angry. 'Oliver's j-jolly brave, so there!'

'I said, some tail,' said the stranger gravely. 'Meaning that it is a very fine large tail and must have belonged to a very large strong rat, and therefore your friend Oliver must be a truly good cat. Who is this Oliver?' he added.

'Why, *he* is,' said Sebastian, pointing to Oliver.

'*Saludos*, Oliver,' said the manx, holding out his paw. 'I'm Scoop, Manx Scoop of *The Cat Times*. Any cat who can bite off a tail like that from a rat like that, is the kind of cat I want to know.'

'Oh?' said Oliver. He was too overcome to be able to think of anything else to say. He extended his paw and Manx Scoop grasped it and gave it a squeeze and a shake which were as great a pain as they were clearly also a compliment.

'Very delighted to meet you, Oliver,' said Manx Scoop. 'Was the fight worthy of the tail?'

'Ra-ther!' said Sebastian. 'The G-General went munch and Oliver went sc-scrunch and there was so much fur f-flying about that I thought, you know, that it had g-gone all f-foggy all of a sudden, and then there were all these rats running away . . .' His voice faded; he had turned shy. Manx Scoop smiled at him very kindly. 'So you were there too? Well done. Another friend for me. What's your name?'

'Seb-bastian.'

'*Saludos*, Sebastian.'

Manx Scoop and Sebastian shook paws.

'So,' said Manx Scoop. 'I understand that you Power Station cats have a Guv'nor. Where is he?'

'Gone to the market to get fish,' said Oliver. 'At least, that's the idea. He should be back very soon.'

'Excellent,' said Manx Scoop. 'Until he returns I will take a stroll by the river. When he returns I will have a word with him if I may. *Saludos amigos.*' And off went Manx Scoop.

'G-goodness!' said Sebastian, tenderly licking his right paw. 'Talk about a sq-sq-sq . . .'

'Squeeze,' said Oliver. 'Me too. Agony.'

The Guv'nor soon returned from the market, carrying an enormous smoked haddock. Behind him came Selina and Ninette, each with a pair of kippers and behind them staggered Nosher and Boney with a box of dried sprats.

'Fish ahoy! Fish ahoy!' chortled the Guv'nor, putting down the haddock. 'No sign of the General, I suppose?'

'None. But there's a character called Manx Something-or-other wanting to see you,' said Oliver.

'Never heard of him.'

'Wot's he like?' asked Selina.

'Great big old cat; eat.you with his early morning milk,' said Oliver.

'Ooh, he wouldn't!' squealed Selina.

At this point Manx reappeared. He said, 'Well, friend Oliver, and which of these toilers of the sea is your Guv'nor?'

Oliver introduced Manx to the Guv'nor. Manx explained, 'I'm from *The Cat Times* and have my nose pressed hard on the trail of a red-hot story of the most fantastic nature, and I believe that you may be in a position to make some shocking disclosures. In other words, I'm covering the story of a crime that's got Scotland Yard and the Feline Flying Squad both tied up in knots and I'm wondering if you, with your . . . er . . . shall we say, distinguished underworld connections, can help me.'

'Depends what you're after,' said the Guv'nor, warily.

'Cat-thief, so far unidentified,' answered Manx. 'And no newcomer to the game, either, to judge by the way he works.'

'There's plenty of cat-thieves around these days,' said the Guv'nor. 'It's a paying game. But the most famous of 'em all, at least in these parts, is Wilberforce Pike.'

At the mention of this name the other cats, with the exception of Manx Scoop, began to scowl and hiss. 'Yeah!' yowled Nosher. 'That old red-sprouting fun-fur! I'd like to fun-fur 'im, I would, straight up!'

'You know him?' asked Manx.

63

'I should cocoa!' said Selina.

'Us lot knows that geezer's strength orright,' grinned Nosher. 'First hand, too.'

'Really?' said Manx.

'He had us lot lagged,' said Nosher. 'But the Guv and old Scratch, they sprung us; least, the Guv did his best and old Scratch pulled it off. Else we'd be fun-furs now. Which might be fun for the wearer, but not much fun for us.'

'You don't love Mr Pike?' queried Manx, sweetly.

'There's not a cat here wouldn't give his teeth and whiskers to settle with that Wilberforce,' replied the Guv'nor, grimly.

'I sense that I've come to the right quarter,' said Manx. 'I had a hunch that you and your Power Station gang might have something useful to say on this matter. So, let us talk.'

'What about having a bit of dinner with us while we're talking?' suggested the Guv'nor. 'There's fish galore and we've a cellar full of catnip. The lads knocked off a load from a brewer's wagon not long since,' he added.

'Dinner,' said Manx, 'is a truly interesting and worthwhile subject to get one's teeth into.' He eyed the sprats as he spoke.

Without more ado catnip was fetched, the fish divided into portions and the rest of the Power Station cats called to the feast. Manx was introduced to everyone; then he sat down to eat, placed between the Guv'nor and Scratch. Over a lengthy and very satisfying repast the reporter was given a detailed account of Wilberforce Pike.

When he had heard all that the Power Station cats had to tell him, Manx asked for permission to refill his glass, took a long hard drink, then began talking in his turn.

'All that you have told me is very valuable. I don't suppose you have much time for reading newspapers or that you hang around police stations, otherwise you'd know that a certain Lollia Paulina has been stolen *en route* to the Cat Show. There's a twenty-five pound reward offered.'

'Offered for what?' said the Guv'nor.

'The recovery of Lollia Paulina.'

'Twenty-five pound for a lost lollypop. Whew!' said the Guv'nor. 'That's a real lot.' He paused, sucked a sprat-tail thoughtfully. 'Twenty-five pounds of what?' he asked, finally.

'Why, twenty-five pounds,' replied Manx.

'Yes, but pounds of *what*? Sprats, butter, pigs' trotters, *what*?'

'Pound notes, you chump,' said Scratch. 'Flimsies, pieces of paper.'

'Blimey, human money! That'll be a lotta good to us cats! What would a cat like me do with pieces of human paper-money?'

'Change it into cat currency; then go into a cat shop and buy things,' said Manx.

'I've never bought anything in my life yet; live by stealing, I do mate, and proud of it. Never stooped to buying yet, and I hope I never have to,' retorted the Guv'nor indignantly.

'Orright,' said Scratch, laughing, 'you stick to your code, Guv, but I daresay the rest of us wouldn't say no to twenty-five quid.'

'I don't see what this has got to do with us, anyway,' said the Guv'nor, rather pettishly. 'Nor with Pikey, neither. What'd Wilberforce Pike be doing, wasting his time pinching a perishing lollypop? Cats is what he nicks, not sweetmeats.'

'I see that I haven't made myself clear,' said Manx. 'Lollia Paulina is a cat; a champion Siamese queen with a pedigree long as that lengthy tail hanging on the wall there.' He nodded at the General's tail. 'And whoever it was stole her must have been a very cool operator, a very cool operator indeed.'

'How'd it happen?' asked Scratch.

'Her Highness was lifted, complete with basket, from the arrival platform at Euston station, during the bare couple of minutes in which her owner was finding a porter. A very neat theft; done in a trice.'

'Sounds like Pikey. He's an old hand who'd never let an opportunity miss,' said Nosher.

'Sounds very much like him,' said Albert. 'That's how he nicked – I mean – stole me,' he added. He cleared his throat impressively. 'I was being taken to the vet; nothing much, simply a small splinter in the paw; came out of its own accord a few days later, but that's neither here nor there. The crux of my story is that I was on the way to the vet; I was in a basket on the passenger seat of the car, a Morris one-thousand, second-hand, but still, mark you, in excellent condition, and . . .'

'Oh, cut it out, Albert!' groaned Selina. 'Jus' say wot happened and get a move on!'

'I *am* saying what happened!' retorted Albert. 'I was in my basket, in the car, and this pestiferous Pike personage spotted me, opened the car door, cool as you please, lifted out my basket with me inside and walked off – just like that. It simply took my breath away.'

'I'll bet it was the old red-sprouter wot grabbed this Lollypop,' said Scratch. 'Job's got his dabs all over it, if you ask me.'

'Yeah, it'll be Wilberforce orright,' agreed all the other cats in chorus.

'So what now?' said Scratch. 'Do we leave things to you Mr Scoop, or do we rescue this 'ere Lollypop ourselves? I mean, for twenty-five flimsies it's worth it.'

'Real bit of fat, to rescue a cat; I wouldn't care what I did, for twenty-five quid,' declared Nosher.

'If you lot could rescue her on your own it would make one hell of a story,' mused Manx Scoop. ' "Former Victims of Catdom's Enemy Number One Strike Back!" Yes, it's a honey. Question is, can you do it?'

'I don't see why not,' said Scratch. 'Give it a try, anyway.'

'We'll have this 'ere Lollypop sprung in no time, mister, or my name's not Nosher,' added that optimistic animal with one of his famous toothy grins.

'Yeah, and arter that, gettin' old Pikey fixed oughter follow easy,' said Nibs.

'My faith in you is boundless,' said Manx. 'If I may I'll move in here while the operation is in progress; full coverage requires me to be on the spot. You won't find me a nuisance,' he added quickly. 'I've been around and know enough to be useful.'

'That's orright, mate,' said Scratch. 'I can see meself that you got that useful look.'

'Thanks,' said Manx. 'I've lived at least ninety-nine of my nine lives and been prodigal with my fighting allowance, but I've a good battle or two left in me yet, and when the juice is up I'm not to be sniffed at. And now I'll shove back to base and collect a few necessities: my sleeping-bag, tea-kettle and trusty bearer.'

'Trusty what?' asked Oliver, adding politely, 'Please, sir.' There was something about Manx that bred great respect in the young cat.

'Bearer,' said Manx. 'A relic of my great and, alas, distant days as a war correspondent. And now, *amigos*, I depart, but my return will be a speedy one. Thank you for a most delicious feast and some exceedingly excellent catnip. *Adios*.' He bowed very politely to the company and went.

Immediately, the cats began discussing plans to rescue the Lollypop. The first, obvious, step was to confirm that she was indeed within the clutches of Wilberforce and, since there was not a moment of time to waste, Scratch was at once sent off on a reconnaissance of the Pike premises.

After Scratch's departure the other cats finished off every remaining scrap of fish and then curled themselves up among the warm pipes to sleep while they had the chance. Nibs and Albert were placed on guard duty over the General's tail.

After their excellent dinner they found it very difficult to stay awake. Albert, in fact, was swaying on his feet and Nibs had his eyes tight shut when a discreet, yet unmistakable cough, brought them both wide awake with a start.

'What's that?' they each asked the other.

'Listen,' they advised one another.

They stood listening. Behind a pipe something moved.

'Halt!' bellowed Albert. 'Who goes there?'

'That's right, shout the place down!' yelled Nibs, furiously turning upon Albert. 'Now whatever – whoever it was, you've scared 'em off an' that's for sure!'

'Friend,' said a trembling voice.

'I'll give you friend, you clot,' snarled Nibs, livid with Albert.

'Advance friend and give the password,' intoned Albert.

'You gone NUTS?' yowled Nibs, shaking his fist at Albert.

'Ssh,' whispered Albert, who had his eyes fixed in the direction of the pipe, 'here he comes.'

Nibs jerked round to face in the same direction. From

behind the pipe stepped a very stout and most timid-looking black-and-white cat.

'Good evening, gentlemen,' he said, in a plummy voice which trembled in spite of his desperate efforts to control it. 'I'm afraid I don't know the password, but I do indeed assure you that I am a friend.'

'Cheers!' said Nibs, sarcastically. 'We needed one, didn't we, Bert?'

'If you can't give the password I shall have to fire, you know,' said Albert, flourishing a very old and rusty rifle with which he fortified himself whenever he stood guard.

'You got it back to front, mate,' said Nibs, who scorned firearms, relying on his own teeth and claws. 'You shoot with that end,' patting the barrel of the rifle with his paw. 'Pull that ole trigger now an', if she do go off, wham, it'll be you what gets your block blown away, not 'im,' nodding at the stout black-and-white cat, who gave a simpering smile.

'I am perfectly aware which end is which,' snapped Albert, hastily righting his weapon. 'Now, friend, can you give that password, or not?'

'The password,' said Nibs contemptuously, 'is "Hip-hip-hooray, isn't it a lovely day?" Now who are you, and wot you doing sticking your fat old snitch in 'ere?'

'My name is Bylines. Whisky Bylines,' said the black-and-white cat, 'chief crime correspondent for *The Cat Courier*.'

'No crime down 'ere, mister,' said Nibs. 'Law-abiding, us lot down 'ere. 'Sright, innit Albert?'

'Certainly,' boomed Albert. To the visitor he said, 'Are you an authorized person?'

'I told you. I'm Whisky Bylines of the . . .'

'Yes, yes, we heard all that; but have you got a pass, issued by the superintendent of this Power Station, to enter the premises?'

'I have my press-card,' said Whisky, feeling in his pocket.

'No use at all, I'm afraid,' said Albert. 'In fact, quite the reverse.'

'I can't imagine why you say that,' retorted Whisky, much put out. 'I know for a fact that Manx Scoop of *The Cat Times* spent a good couple of hours here earlier on. I watched him come in, and watched him go out. If you can talk to the *Times* I'm sure you can talk to me.'

'Mr Scoop is assisting us with a small professional job we're interested in,' said Albert, loftily.

'Oh, is he? Well, I wouldn't put anything past friend Scoop and that's a fact,' snorted Whisky nastily. 'I always said . . . but never mind.' He fished in another pocket. 'Will *that* help you to feel differently about talking to me?' he added, proffering Albert half a crown in cat money.

'I have never accepted a bribe in my life!' said Albert, in a voice which totally deflated poor Whisky. Nibs peered at the coin in his turn. 'Wot's he offerin' you, Bert? Cor, stone it, perishin' tosheroon! Wot's he think we are? Have to be at least a fiver to talk to a broken down news-cat like 'im.'

'Five hundred wouldn't tempt me. Nor five thousand, neither. Nor five million! Nor billion!' boomed Albert.

'Steady on, Bert, don't want to burn yer boats like that,' said Nibs. 'Bloke was comin' up with offer of five million that very moment, if you'd kept your big mouth shut.'

'I must insist on a little respect,' said Whisky. 'After all, I'm only trying to get a story for my paper; it's nothing personal. I mean I couldn't care less, myself, about this Miss Lily Poona, or whoever she calls herself, being stolen, but my editor thinks it's front-page stuff and so . . .'

'Her Highness Lollia Paulina,' said Albert.

'Oh, you know about her?'

'Naturally.'

'What do you know?'

'That she's been stolen.'

'Oh? Know who has stolen her?' Whisky's tone was eager.

'Sure,' said Nibs.

'Who? Tell me who, my boy. I'll make it worth your while.'

'Why, one of them cat-thief chaps, innit?'

'Yes, yes, but what's his name?'

'Ah, now you're askin'.'

'This,' said Whisky, 'will drive me mad, but raving mad. Haven't you a gang leader; someone responsible I can talk to?'

'Well,' said Nibs, grinning, 'here comes old Scratch. Why not try having a word with him?'

Scratch loped his way towards them. 'Who in the name of flamin' fortune's this?' he said, scowling at Whisky.

'Pipelines or skylines, or somethink or other he calls 'isself,' said Nibs. 'Reporter from *The Cat Courier*. Wants to know 'bout the stolen Lollypop.'

'Well, he can go somewhere else to find out,' snapped Scratch. 'He don't take my fancy.'

'I assure you,' faltered Whisky, clearly alarmed by Scratch, 'I am here on perfectly legitimate journalistic purposes . . .'

'No good usin' them long words on me,' said Scratch. 'Never passed my 'leven plus, I ain't. And now you take a penn'orth, mister, if you know wot's good for you. Go on, or don'tcher talk King's English? I said scram!'

Whisky Bylines tumbled out backwards, terrified. Scratch said, 'Orright, now we're shot of 'im, you go and fetch the others, Nibs, for if we wanta rescue that Lollypop we gotta act real fast.'

8. The Volunteer

'She's there at Pike's orright,' Scratch told the assembled cats. 'I could hear her crying and calling for help; no mistaking her Siamese voice. But how we gonna get her out is another matter; the winder's bin mended, so that way in ain't no good no more; all the other winders of the house is tight shut and we can't bank on anyone being lucky enough to dodge in like I did last time when I sprung you lot.'

'H'm,' said the Guv'nor. 'Doesn't sound too good.'

'It ain't,' said Scratch. 'Old Pikey's took a load of security precautions since you lot crashed out.'

'We gotta think,' said Nosher. 'Gotta think what to do, for the whole scene is new.'

While everyone sat thinking, Manx Scoop returned, accompanied by what looked like a small walking mountain of camping gear. There was a rucksack with mugs, a kettle, a hammer, a spare pair of shoes and a frying-pan dangling from it, hooked on wherever a hook could be contrived; strapped to the top of the rucksack was a groundsheet and on top of this was an enormous bedding-roll and, perched on the summit of this, a minute roll of striped blanket. The mountain had two little brown furry forepaws, one of which grasped a small, battered attaché-case and the other a large wicker picnic basket. Close scrutiny revealed that the mountain had also white cotton baggy trousers tight at the ankles, and weeny oriental feet.

Manx himself was carrying a portable typewriter and had a portable tape-recorder slung by a strap over one shoulder.

'Halt, Ranjit Singh!' said Manx to the mountain. The mountain halted smartly and placed the picnic basket and attaché-case on the ground. Manx then assisted the mountain to divest itself of itself and there, standing in the middle of a pile of camping gear, was a very determined-looking mongoose with a turban tilted crookedly over one eye.

The cats had never seen a mongoose before and they were

71

staring at him with great interest and wondering whatever kind of animal he might be, when Manx Scoop enlightened them. 'Children, this is Ranjit Singh, my faithful mongoose. Ranjit, say "how d'you do" to the sahibs. They are all fighting men and very worthy. Oh, and two of them are members of the stronger sex; it goes without saying that they are very, very worthy.'

Ranjit Singh pressed the pads of his forepaws together, raised them to his forehead thus, and salaam'd deeply to the company. He then straightened his turban.

'Coo, innee cute!' shrilled Selina. The mongoose darted her a look of fire and she collapsed behind Scratch, murmuring, 'Coo, no he ain't!'

Scratch now reported to Manx all that he had already told the other cats about Lollia Paulina and the Pike fortress. Manx listened attentively and at last said, 'So?'

'So we're thinking what's best to do. Searching for brain-waves,' said the Guv'nor.

'And the more we think the less b-brainwavey we f-feel.' said Sebastian.

'Nothing like a think-tank to destroy thought,' said Manx. 'I always find a drink helpful,' he added, hopefully.

'Good idea,' said the Guv'nor. 'Boney, Nibs, fetch out some catnip.'

'Drink and the world drinks with you, think and you think alone,' intoned Albert. 'Not,' he added hastily, 'that this is intended as a criticism of anyone.'

'Of course not,' said Manx. 'However, it is most true. By the way, talking of drinking, was that old Whisky Bylines I saw lurking in the laurels as I came past?'

'It was,' said Nibs. 'Whisky Bylines of *The Cat Courier*.'

'I thought I recognized that urbane brow, that ample paunch. Has he talked to you?'

'He wanted to talk, but he never got nowhere,' said Nibs. 'He tried to bribe old Albert, though.'

'He offered me half a crown,' said Albert. 'I spurned it.'

'Good for you,' said Manx. 'Nevertheless, it's a great pity that he's turned up, as he's liable to be the most awful nuisance. He looks a bit of a mug, but actually that's all my eye; he's a very wily chap indeed and a damn good journalist.'

'He won't get far, not with this story he won't,' said Scratch. 'Don't you fret, Mr Scoop.'

'Adds zest to a job to have a rival on it, of course,' said Manx. 'But this time I must confess I'm more interested in settling accounts with Wilberforce Pike than I am in the pure and simple newspaper angle. After all . . .'

'Wot's that?' interrupted Ninette, cocking her ears.

'What's what?'

'Thought I heard a sorta snuffling noise . . .' She rose and stole to peep behind a pipe. 'No,' she said, shaking her head, 'must've imagined it.' She sat down again.

'Have a drink and try to think,' said Nosher, handing her a glass of catnip. 'With that you ought to get a thought; before very long, too, because it's strong, too.'

'*Skoll!*' said Manx, raising his glass. 'Here's to inspiration!'

'Brainwaves galore!' said Albert, raising his glass.

'And so say all of us!' chorused the rest. They all drank. There was a long silence.

'I g-g-got it! I g-g-got it!' shouted Sebastian, at last.

'I have got it,' said Albert, loudly.

'First come first served; can't both talk at once,' said Scratch. 'So young Seb, spill the beans; tell us wot you got.'

'A b-brainwave,' said Sebastian. 'Rescuing the L-Lolly-p-p-pop. Must be done like this. Somebody – the Guv'nor or Nosher, or somebody – gets caught by P-Pike accidental-done-on-purpose, and p-put inside, and he p-p-picks all the locks and lets himself and the L-Lollyp-pop out, and there you are. B-Bob's your uncle!'

'Blimey, young Seb, that's genius, that is!' said Boney.

All the cats chorused approval.

'Now let's hear Albert's idea, and then we'll choose which-ever is best,' said Scratch.

They all looked expectantly at Albert.

'I have got no idea, I'm afraid,' said Albert.

'But you said you had.'

'I didn't you know.'

'But we all heard you say you'd got it!'

'I have got it,' said Albert. 'Not I got it, but I have got it.

I have not got it. I have it. I have had it. Have you had it? Have you got it? What have you got?'

'Strewth!' said Scratch.

'A little matter of grammatical know-how,' said Albert. 'That was all. I had not actually got anything. I wish that I had had. It might have been helpful. Had I had anything I would have let you hear it, of course. But whatever you do do, think it out well first.'

'The had hads and the do do's always give me the peejy-weejies,' said Manx Scoop. 'Let's get back to young Sebastian's idea and see if we think it'll go.'

So they concentrated hard on Sebastian's idea and the more they talked about it the better it seemed.

'Who's best at picking locks?'

'Old Scratch is.'

'Yes, but s'pose he can't get out, then who's going to spring him? You wanta keep Scratch in reserve. You don't want your best cracksman shoved in chokey.'

'Who's next best at picking locks?'

'Boney, Nibs, the Guv'nor.'

'Bags I volunteer to be caught,' said the Guv'nor.

'Guv, you've got bags of guts and you mean well, but trouble is you always goof things up so.'

'Not this time I won't; give you my word,' said the Guv'nor.

'Say that every time, Guv.'

'This time'll be different, I promise you.'

So it was agreed. The Guv'nor was to be caught by Pike. He was to have suitable lock-picking gear hidden about his person and, once caged at the Pike residence, was at the first opportunity to pick his lock, leap from his cage, free Lollia Paulina and any other cats imprisoned there, and they would then make good their escape.

'Now all we gotta do is find out which part of town old Pike's a-workin' at present,' said Boney.

Their plans laid, a merry party was soon in full swing. Nibs was sent to bring more catnip, and then more catnip again; this last time he returned out of breath, and very excited.

'I say, we're in luck! He's prowlin' around outside now!'

'Who is?'

'Pikey! He's got his sack an' his cat-basket, and his flippin' phoney tail danglin' at the ready!'

All the other cats cheered.

'First time on record any cat's bin glad to see the old red-sprouter!' laughed Scratch.

The Guv'nor stood up. 'Where's the wire for the lock-picking?'

Scratch produced a suitable piece of wire and this the Guv'nor concealed twisted round one leg and hidden by his fur. 'Well, so long folks, I'm off,' he said, trying to sound casual.

'So long, me old china,' said Scratch, patting him warmly on the shoulder. 'Remember to look before you leap, an' all that jazz. That there wire's for you to let yourself and the lady out wiv, not for strangling yerself, and if you're not home and dry by dinner-time tomorrer, we'll know you've goofed it again. Only remember this, Guv; old Pikey's battened down his hatches and it's gonna be a lot harder to spring you this time.'

'Trust me; this job'll go without a hitch. Right on the ball, that's me, boy; right on the ball,' said the Guv'nor.

'Okey-doke, double-o-seven, off you go,' said Scratch. 'An' good luck.'

Amidst the cheers and back-slapping of the other cats away went the Guv'nor on his mission.

The night was foggy, the shrubbery thick with gloom as he crept through it. Somewhere in the fog prowled Wilberforce Pike, sack-festooned, cat-seeking. Now, while he stalked his prey, the Guv'nor stalked him; soon discovering where Wilberforce skulked, behind a privet hedge by the river bank. The Guv'nor crept stealthily towards the cat-snatcher, picking his silent way between winter-bare branches; there was an open patch of grass a few yards from where Pike lurked and there the Guv'nor planned to show himself. But, as he stole forward, a fat shape glided up to him with surprising speed and a throaty voice purred in his ear, 'Excuse me, may I have one quick word?'

'No, not now,' hissed the Guv'nor.

'I assure you, not more than a second. An interview for the *Courier*.'

'Beat it.'

'Just one question. I *understand* that you are about to allow yourself to be captured by . . . er . . . Palmerston Spike in an attempt to rescue Princess Polly Loona. Can you let me know, in a few succinct words; what does it feel like to walk into the jaws of fate with your eyes open?'

'I don't know what you're talking about.'

'Aren't you on the point of letting yourself be caught?'

'If you let me let meself get caught mister, instead of wasting my time with tom-fool questions.'

'Marvellous! Marvellous! How I admire courage! What a story!' gushed Whisky. He shut his eyes for a second. 'I can see it; bannerline: "The cat who dared to risk death to expose a villain". Now, please, in a few quick words; won't detain you a brace of shakes: what are your thoughts, your feelings, at this moment of moments? Will you address the Princess as Your Royal Highness, or be democratic and simply call her Polly? How do you propose to spend the reward money? What do you think of space exploration? Should cats take part in it?'

'Oh, get out of my way!'

'I understand that you have a piece of wire with which you intend to pick the locks . . .'

'How *do* you know all this?'

'My job, my dear boy, my job to ferret out facts.'

'Ferret! A dirty eavesdropping rat, that's what you are! Now I know who it was Ninette heard sniffing behind that pipe!'

'All's fair in love and war, Mr Goofy.'

'Make war not love, that's my motto!' hissed the Guv'nor. 'You wait till I get back from this Lollypop lark; I'll chew you to mincemeat!'

And he shook a furious paw in Whisky's face, then rushed away into the fog, while Whisky muttered 'Whew!' sat down hard and mopped his forehead with a silk handkerchief.

The Guv'nor, meanwhile, raced forward in his eagerness to waste no more time and hurled himself on to the empty patch of grass in front of Wilberforce, appearing rather like a conjurer's cat from nowhere. Wilberforce almost startled out of his skin. 'Cor, blimey!' He clutched at his sack and stared at the cat. 'Where you sprung from? Gimme a proper turn!'

The Guv'nor, still scowling from his encounter with Whisky, switched on what was intended as a winning smile. Wilberforce eyed him with singular lack of enthusiasm. 'Nasty,

scraggy-looking beast. Don't fancy him. All skin and bone. Wouldn't surprise me if he was mangy, too.'

'Mangy!' spat the Guv'nor outraged. 'Mangy yourself!'

'Spits like a bad-tempered kettle!' said Wilberforce. 'Nasty animal that, altogether. I won't burden myself with him.'

And he turned on his heel and lurched off into the fog.

The Guv'nor, horrified, galloped after Wilberforce, mewing, 'Catch me! For heaven's sake, catch me!'

Wilberforce was wearing rubber-soled shoes and, like all professional thieves, he moved very silently. The Guv'nor soon lost track of him in the gloom. The cat searched in frantic circles, upbraiding himself under his breath, 'You chump, you twit, you looney! Goofed it again! Goofed it again!'

9. Second Time Round

Oliver found the catnip very powerful and the cats' lair very stuffy, so he went outside for a reviving breath of fresh air. By now, he mused, the dear old Guv would be jolting along, for sure, in that unspeakable sack of Wilberforce Pike's. Good old Guv. Dear, brave, decent old Guv'nor Goofer! How like him to volunteer for such a dreadfully dangerous adventure: and to make light of it, too!

The catnip had turned Oliver very sentimental. He crouched beneath a laurel, stared at the fog and thought most fondly of Guv'nor Goofer.

A plump, but firm paw landed on his shoulder. 'One of the Power Station gang? An exclusive interview for the *Courier*: won't take a jiffy. What do you feel about your heroic leader? Will this splendid example he is setting you young gangsters change your attitudes, your way of life? Why did you take to crime? Are you on drugs? Do you smoke catnip; are you hooked on caterpills?'

A round, black-and-white face pushed itself against Oliver's; long whiskers tickled his nose; he stared in amazement into jade-green eyes.

'Have you had any court-convictions? Are you ex-Cat-Borstal? What is your opinion of the Royal Feline Fuzz? Don't be afraid to talk: you won't be named or photographed. In a few simple sentences, what would your thoughts be if you found yourself captured by Wilberforce . . . Help!'

A great human hand appeared; Whisky vanished.

Oliver looked up. As if in a nightmare he saw that huge red face, that gleaming stark bald head, those vast purple ears, those sprouts of carroty hair. Then he, too, was grasped, lifted, stuffed headlong into that nightmare sack. He found himself impossibly mixed up with the frantically mewing and struggling Whisky. Then there was much jolting and the old, all-too-well-remembered sensation of sickening terror.

The Guv'nor, who had charged round the corner of the laurel thicket in time to see Whisky animatedly talking to Oliver, had next glimpsed a shadow, a movement, a gaping of a swiftly opened sack, two struggling figures seized and dropped into it. Their cries very quickly stifled, to be followed by a hideous human chuckle. Then Pike's big baggy figure was swallowed by swirling fog.

The Guv'nor, in a near-state of collapse, tumbled back to the other cats. For several moments they could make nothing of his demented mewing. But at last they grasped the sobering message: Oliver and Whisky Bylines, neither of whom had lock-picking gear, had been captured and carried off by Pike, while the Guv'nor, complete with his escape wire, had been left to run free.

'What a mess!' groaned Scratch.

'He said I was mangy. A burden. I mewed. I begged him to take me. I pretty near climbed up his legs!'

'It's gonna be the devil's own job to get 'em back. That house has bin turned into a real security joint.'

'I ran round and round looking for him; praying for him to take me.'

'You really have made a muck of things this time, Guv.'

'I know. I know. Oh, I could tear myself to bits, I really could!'

Oliver was not at first recognized by Wilberforce: it took Mrs Pike to realize who he was. 'Why, it's that young Gospo agin!'

'So it is!' said Wilberforce, peering into the cat-basket, prior to transferring Oliver into a cage. 'What a coincidence!'

'Well, he won't be getting no nice coley out of me this time. Dee-hy-drated-mouse and water; that's all for 'im this time round,' said Mrs Pike. 'Ungrateful wretch; chewing a lump outa my thumb.'

Oliver noticed, to his immense satisfaction, that she still wore a thumb-stall.

'He won't be staying long enough this time to need nothing to eat,' said Wilberforce. 'I'm selling 'em tomorrer.'

'You must be daft if you're gonna sell that Siamese,' said

Mrs Pike, nodding in the direction of a cage across the room. Oliver craned his neck and glimpsed creamy fur, black pointed ears, huge china blue eyes, seductively squinting and aslant. 'You'll not get more than a few quid for selling her; while there's twenty-five going as a reward to anyone who returns her to her missis.'

'Yeah; an' if I return her there'll be all them awkward questions asked: where'd I find her, how'd I lay hands on her; where's she bin between vanishing from Euston and being handed back to her mistress at the Ritz. Next thing I know, I'll 'ave the coppers round.'

'They'll be round here one of these fine days in any case,' said Mrs Pike.

'Think it's time we hopped the twig, eh? Found ourselves another gaff?' said Wilberforce.

'You're dead right,' said his lady. 'I do.'

'Female hintuition ain't to be sniffed at,' observed Wilberforce thoughtfully. 'We done so well lately it's time we could afford to give ourselves a nice change of air.'

'If we don't give ourselves one, somebody else will!'

'True, true my love.'

'A pony would be very useful. Help take us to the seaside.'

'It certainly would. I'll 'ave a little think about it arter supper.'

Oliver was so interested in this conversation, even if he did not understand all of it, that he allowed himself to be transferred to a cage without protest.

Whisky, however, made a great nuisance of himself, scratching and biting and declaring in a high-pitched voice that this outrage would become a front-page story in the *Courier*, and every animal in catdom would be after Wilberforce's blood. Since, however, neither Mr nor Mrs Pike spoke cat-language, these threats had little effect upon them.

At last the Pikes went downstairs to their supper and Oliver and Whisky found themselves alone with the Siamese prisoner. She was indeed a seductive and delicious creature; even when distraught, squeezed into a dirty little cage, she was beautiful and her great cerulean eyes made Oliver feel quite dizzy. His emotions at finding himself captured again, together with the overwhelming presence of the Siamese, rendered him speechless.

Whisky, however, after a struggle, got himself sufficiently under control to ask, 'Excuse me, madam, but have I the pleasure of addressing the celebrated Highness Lonnie Pooley?'

She shook her head with a disdainful expression.

'Drat it,' muttered Whisky. 'Got it wrong. How damn unprofessional!' He breathed hard, then tried again. 'Pollo Lol . . .?'

'Princess Lollia Paulina,' said Oliver.

'Yes?' said the Princess, flicking her left ear rapidly and opening her eyes very wide.

'Allow me to introduce myself,' put in Whisky. 'Bylines, Whisky Bylines; special correspondent of *The Cat Courier*.'

'Really?' said the Princess distantly, while giving Whisky a glance that was not friendly.

'I have been assigned to cover your story.'

'Oh?' Distinctly, she was not enchanted.

'Your feelings at being captured; your hopes . . .'

'Oh shut up, Whisky Bylines. We can't afford the luxury of newspaper twiddle-twaddle now,' snapped Oliver, surprising himself by his boldness. He turned to the Princess. 'How long have you been a prisoner here, please, Princess?'

'Four days.' The Princess added, with interest, 'What is your name?'

'Oliver Simpkin.' He hurried on, 'Have you had any other cats here with you?'

'There were six when I arrived, but he, that horrible man, took them away; he sold them, I think. They were in a terrible state; they seemed to think they were going to be made into fur coats! Surely that can't be true?'

'Perfectly true, I'm afraid,' said Oliver. 'Fun-furs.'

'Oh no!' She gazed at him wildly. 'Oh, poor things, poor things!'

'Surely not!' quivered Whisky. 'I mean, these days they use nylon.'

'Not for all fun-furs. Bunnies and cats are used for some.

'Bunnies, oh well. Stupid creatures,' said Whisky contemptuously. 'But cats; that's scandalous. An outrage. And in a civilized country! No, I don't believe it.'

'I've been here before,' said Oliver. 'I know what Pike's game is. Fun-furs we'll finish up as, unless the Guv'nor and Scratch and that lot get here pretty quick.'

'Oh no, oh no!' moaned the Princess.

'You've got a chance, Princess. You heard what he said, he may take you back to your owner and claim the reward.'

'Oh, he's been waffling about that for days now. First he'll sell me, then he'll return me to my mistress and get the twenty-five pounds! Oh if only he would return me to her! I don't think he means to, though; he has taken away my collar with my name and address on it!'

'What happened to that Guv'nor Goofer? Why isn't he here?' asked Whisky, peevishly. 'He was going to let himself be caught so that he could rescue the Princess, remember? I had a terrific interview with him on the strength of it. Cold feet at the last moment, I suppose.'

'Cold feet? The good old Guv'nor? That's one thing he'd never get. He may be a goofer, but he's no coward.'

'Then why isn't he here?' sneered Whisky.

'Because no doubt he goofed it,' replied Oliver, glumly.

'Rescue?' exclaimed the Princess, pricking her ears. 'Is there going to be a rescue?'

'There was a lot of talk,' said Whisky. 'No do, I'm afraid. Like all these young chaps of today, they've no guts when it comes to the crunch.'

'Don't you dare insult my mates!' spat Oliver.

'Mates, indeed!' sniffed Whisky. 'Rag-tag-and-bobtail collection of strays.'

'Ignore him, Oliver,' crooned the Princess. 'Just tell me about this rescue plan, please.'

So Oliver told her.

'What a brave cat your Guv'nor Goofer must be!' she sighed.

'Biggest chump-headed ass in creation, if you ask me!' mewed Whisky.

'But we aren't asking you, Mr Bylines,' purred the Princess. She turned her blue gaze back to Oliver. 'Do you think there is any chance of our still being rescued, Oliver? You don't mind me calling you Oliver, do you?'

Oliver, quite overcome, stammered as if he were Sebastian. 'Oh, p-please do!'

'Do you think, then, that they will still try to rescue us, Oliver?'

'Well . . .' Oliver reflected. 'The Guv'nor isn't here, so that means he wasn't stolen by Pike. And that means that he's still at the Power Station. And before long they'll discover that I've disappeared and so they may, they *should*, put two-and-two together and realize that I've been stolen instead of the Guv'-nor. And the Guv'nor being what he is, and Scratch what he is they'll organize a rescue right away. But as Scratch pointed out when they were planning to rescue you in the first place, this is no easy joint to bust these days.'

'I'm sorry, I didn't quite understand that last bit.'

'This is not an easy house to get into,' explained Oliver.

So the Princess and Oliver talked, all through the long night, about the chances of rescue and then he told her all about his previous imprisonment and rescue and about his life before he had been stolen and about his present life at the Power Station, and she listened beautifully, flicking her ear when she became really interested, her eyes growing bigger and bigger.

'Oh, *poor* Guv'nor Goofer, catching his foot in the curtain like that! And Scratch, what a wonderfully clever, resourceful ani-mal he must be! Oh I *would* like to meet your friends so much!'

'Hm hrrmph!' from Whisky's cage.

The night passed. Morning came; Mrs Pike brought meagre portions of fish and milk to the Princess, merely water to Whisky and Oliver. This struck great terror into these two cats, for it meant that Pike must intend selling them very soon. Perhaps, the Princess at all events was going to be returned to her mistress? But she said that she was tòo miserable and frightened about the fate of Oliver to care what happened to her. Oh, and of course one didn't want poor Mr Bylines turned into a fun-fur either.

The caged cats suffered tortures of fear, hunger, cold and cramp, hour after long hour.

The master of the house made no appearance. Mrs Pike

could be heard from time to time moving about in the kitchen. She had the wireless on; it played jarring, cheerful music.

Wilberforce Pike, at mid-morning, found himself walking across the foyer of a fine and elegant and very expensive hotel, and asking for Mrs Cartmel-Coniston-Cartmel-Carr. The receptionist looked at Wilberforce doubtfully. He explained huskily and quickly, 'Name of Smithers. I've come about a missin' cat.' The receptionist telephoned Mrs Cartmel-Coniston-Cartmel-Carr's suite to inform her of her visitor and within moments Wilberforce found himself seated on a handsome sofa in a room full of flowers, talking to a fragile-seeming, grey-haired woman, who 'scared the living daylights' out of Pike, as he was later to admit to his wife.

He repeated, nervously, the tale that he had rehearsed over and over again all the way to the Ritz. How he had found this Siamese cat wandering, mewing and hungry, along Euston Road. How he, a great cat lover, had taken her home and fed her on chicken and salmon – 'I could see she was used to the best'. How he and his wife had quite fallen in love with the cat who was 'sweet as 'oney and good as gold'. How they had heard about the vanished champion Siamese and realized that their new-found pet must be the very same. How Mrs Pike, though it broke her heart, had insisted that the cat must be returned to her rightful mistress; 'The reward don't come into it; my thoughts are all with that pore woman frettin' over wot's become of her darlin' cat.' And so, concluded Wilberforce, here he was.

'But where is my cat?'

'Well you see, madam, I wanted to make sure it was your cat before I hactually fetched her along. You see, you might 'ave got your cat back, and then this cat wot I got wouldn't be your cat arter all, would it?'

'I don't see how she could be my cat. Mine was stolen complete with basket. Besides, mine wore a collar bearing her name and address. You would be in no doubt if she were my cat.'

'The thief musta took that collar orf of 'er; first thing he'd do, ma'am. As for the basket; she'd managed to get out of that and escape from him. She's your cat orright; answers in every detail to your hadvertised description.'

'The only way to settle the problem is to bring the cat here as soon as possible.'

'I'll 'ave her along 'ere by two o'clock this afternoon.'

'I will be waiting.'

'And there'll be this reward?'

'Certainly, if she is my cat.'

'Oh, she'll be your cat orright.'

'I still don't understand how she came to be wandering in the Euston Road.'

'She managed to hescape from the thief wot stole 'er, that's wot.'

'Have you been to the police about this? We should try to catch this terrible man.'

'I ain't bin yet, but I will,' lied Wilberforce, who had no more intention of going near a police-station than of visiting Timbuctoo.

'I'll contact the police, too. We must catch this man.'

'Yus, yus,' said Wilberforce, leaping up from the sofa. 'I'll be orf now to get your cat.'

'This cat-stealing is a dreadfully wicked thing, Mr Smithers.'

'It certainly is!' agreed Wilberforce, heartily.

'May I have your address, please, I might need it,' said Mrs Cartmel-Coniston-Cartmel-Carr.

'Sixteen Boot Mansions.' Having given this false address he rattled on quickly, hoping to divert her attention from him. 'Oh, stealing a cat is downright wicked! Like stealing part of somebody's 'eart, stealing their cat is! I'd . . . well, I don't know what I'd do to any man I caught cat-stealing. Can't think of any punishment bad enough.'

And with this speech Mr Pike hurried away.

'I shan't be taking pussy back there, reward or no reward. Find meself in the flowery before I can say wink; not worth it for twenty-five quid,' muttered Wilberforce, who had other things on his conscience besides cat-stealing. If the police did catch him he could expect a very long prison sentence. 'I'll sell them three pussies this arternoon,' Wilberforce promised himself. 'Then if the cops do come searchin' my premises, at least they won't find no hot cats.'

Mrs Pike, meantime, having spent the morning doing household chores, had sat down at last to a cup of instant-coffee and a bath-bun. She had scarcely got her teeth into the bun when there was a double-knock on the front door. Sighing, she went to answer it. She opened the door and immediately a deluge of cats poured upon her. She screamed and tried to drive them back, but they ignored her and galloped into her kitchen. Several rushed up the stairs, one jumped on her shoulder and waved his tail in her eyes. And more and more cats still came scampering in; they waltzed in circles, darted between her feet, played catch-as-catch-can amongst the furniture, clawed the curtains, got into the larder, sent all the pots and pans flying in the scullery. She chased them dementedly, shrieking, 'Shoo!' They capered mockingly round her, doing hand stands and catherine-wheels. The house was alive with mewing cats, behaving as if they were crazy. Then, just as she was about to flee the place, leaving them to it, they all raced out as suddenly as they had come in, and vanished up the street.

Mrs Pike collapsed on to a chair. When Wilberforce got home she was still in such a state she could not properly tell him what had happened. 'Cats, cats, cats! All the cats in the world come here! Ooh, you shoulda seen 'em, Pikey! Runnin' here, runnin' there, mewing and miaowing . . .'

'Wot you bin up to, eh?' said Wilberforce unkindly. 'These days you're always seeing things. First it's pink rats, then it's mad cats. Like I shall think it's the hoo-ha's you got if you see anythink else.'

'They was real, Pikey. I swear they was real!'

'Well, real or not, I ain't got time to bother. I gotta get them three stolen cats sold pronto if I don't wanta land in the cooler!' And upstairs hurried Wilberforce, to come tumbling down again two minutes later with the news that all three cages had been opened and their occupants were gone.

10. Blue Daffodils

Back at the Power Station tremendous jollifications were taking place. All the cats were dancing to music played by Twinkey on a piano-accordion. Manx Scoop had sent out for a crate of champagne; corks were popping, there was laughter and singing. The Princess, radiant, danced cat two-steps, twists and cha-cha-cha's with thrilled partner after partner. Selina spun round and round with her beloved Scratch, making sure that he did not have more than one dance with the Princess, who had obviously made a terrific impression upon him. Ninette taught Albert, who only knew how to Old-Tyme-Dance, the intricate movements of the cat-tango. Ranjit Singh performed, solo, something peculiar and frenzied, which he called a Punjabi Reel. Whisky Bylines was given one turn round the floor by the Princess (who clearly still did not think much of him); she then returned to her other partners. She tried a two-step with the Guv'nor, but he tripped and sent them both sprawling; she was very sweet about it, but the Guv'nor was so ashamed and overcome that he fled and hid himself amongst the laurels, where he huddled in misery, stricken by a fearful migraine. Whisky, too, soon left the party; he went home to his flat and his typewriter.

By three in the morning the party began to flag a little; the Princess asked for catmint-tea. This refined delicacy was unknown to the Power Station cats; Nosher, however, raided the staff canteen and returned with a packet of something labelled 'Cosy Kuppa'. Ranjit Singh, who had been seated cross-legged in a corner with his eyes closed, chanting a very long, monotonous Sikh song to himself, rose abruptly, scuttled across to Nosher, seized the packet of Cosy Kuppa and hissed, 'Sahib, Sahib, are you out of your senses? Would you insult a high-born personage such as the Princess with *this*?'

'It's tea, innit?'

'Tea!' spluttered the mongoose. 'It will make hot dirty liquid tasting like Scoop Sahib's bathwater!'

'It's what they all drink in the staff canteen.'

'Ugh! No wonder these English are the colour of old washing-up cloths! Take it back to where you found it, Mr Nosher, I implore you, please.'

'But the Princess wants tea.'

'She shall have it. I myself will prepare her either some of Scoop Sahib's best Darjeeling, four shillings the quarter-pound, or his Lapsang Souchong. But that Cosy Kuppa, Mr Nosher, never!'

So saying, the mongoose hurried off to find Manx Scoop's picnic basket, from which he swiftly took tea things, while the abashed Nosher carried the Cosy Kuppa back to the canteen cupboard.

The Guv'nor returned to find his gangsters seated in a circle round the Princess, all daintily sipping Lapsang Souchong. If some did not think much of it, they were too polite to say so. The mongoose approached the Guv'nor. 'Will you have some tea, Goofer Sahib?'

The Guv'nor was staring at the Princess. With her slender figure, long long black legs, pointed black nose, black pricked ears, creamy body and shining Siamese eyes, blue as the bluest waters, bright as the brightest skies, she was sheer witchery. Goofer Sahib found himself with a tea-cup in his hand, gulping Lapsang Souchong, without the faintest notion either of what he was holding or what he was drinking.

The Princess was chattering animatedly about the rescue. 'It was such a terribly clever idea! I mean, the front-door in broad daylight and all of you together, so that that dreadful woman didn't know which of you to catch first! Who was it thought of such a brilliant scheme?'

'The Guv'nor!' mewed all the cats.

'Oh! I do think it was so fabulous of you to think up such a wonderful rescue!' cried the Princess, turning the full glow of her blue eyes upon the Guv'nor. 'How I do admire BRAINS!' He dropped his teacup. It splintered into atoms.

'My cherished Wedgwood!' groaned Manx. 'However, forget it. Tonight is a night when teacups don't signify.'

The Guv'nor didn't know where to look. The mongoose brought him fresh tea; the Guv'nor took it as if in a trance.

The Princess was still talking gaily. 'I can't honestly remember much about any of it very clearly. A lot of noise; then seeing one of you . . . Oh, which one was it? At the door of my cage, unpicking the lock . . .'

'It was the Guv wot unlocked you,' said Nosher.

'So brave! So clever and brave! Oh, I can never say thank you enough for saving my life; never say thank you enough!' Again she turned her ravishing glance towards the Guv'nor who, now blind and dizzy, stepped forward in a desperate attempt to keep his cool. 'Don't mention it, Lollypopress. May I get you some more tea?'

Her ear flickered. 'Oh thank you. How very kind!'

He advanced, caught the toe of one hind paw in the heel of the other, stumbled, struck his elbow, emptied the contents of his own teacup over the Princess, felt the cup slip from his suddenly dead grasp, heard a second shivering of porcelain, followed by a blood-curdling howl from Manx:

'My dear chap, this isn't a crockery smashing contest, you know!'

Everyone fussed and exclaimed, with the exception of the Princess who remained perfectly tranquil, merely remarking that it didn't matter one little bit that she had tea all over her fur. Someone, furiously indignant with the Guv'nor and his clumsy behaviour, gave him an ungentle kick. 'Clothead!'

The mongoose seized the silver teapot; there was a cry of pain. Twinkey was cowering on the floor, clasping his head. The mongoose lowered the teapot.

'Goofer Sahib is not a clot-head; he is a very fine sahib indeed, but without luck. He suffers many misfortunes; this does not make him a clot-head. There are clot-heads here, but they are not to be found upon Goofer Sahib's shoulders. *You* are a clot-head for calling him one,' said Ranjit Singh severely to Twinkey. 'Next time I will resort to a weapon more serious than my teapot.'

'*My* teapot, Ranjit Singh!' said Manx, loudly.

'Sahib, my great indignation led me to slipshod speech,' said Ranjit Singh. He inspected the teapot. 'Providentially, I have not dented it,' he added.

The Princess watched this little scene with interest; again an ear flickered.

Then she turned to the Guv'nor. A ravishing smile. 'Poor Goofer Sahib, you *do* have bad luck, don't you? Never mind, I'm sure that if Mr Scoop forgives you then I do.'

The Guv'nor tried to speak but could not. She went on, 'I hope you haven't hurt yourself! Did you hit your elbow? Are you feeling all right? You look rather pale.'

'I feel . . . fine. Perfectly fine. Just a slight touch of migraine.'

'Oh, poor *you*. I get them occasionally. Only teeny-weeny ones, but even then they're horrid. Do sit down. Have some more tea; it will make you feel better. Ranjit Singh, more tea for Goofer Sahib!'

Since the Guv'nor was incapable of speech she talked for him; chattering about her mistress (to whom she was returning after the party) and her home in the mountains of the far North. 'It is so beautiful. The air is like wine. There is a huge, blue lake like a sea and the blue mountains soar into the sky all round it. Great clouds float in the sky. In the spring the green slopes under the trees are thick with daffodils. It is the most wonderful place in the world. A magic place.'

She talked of huge birds that soared, mewing like cats; of black ravens that lived for over a hundred years and knew all the secrets of the past; of gold and silver buried in the rocks; of the stars that sang at night and the cuckoos that, in springtime, chimed all day, and of streams that ran carolling down the mountainsides for ever. Of summer bracken which clad the fellsides in rippling seas of green, and of winter snow and ice which made the whole landscape shine. The cats listened spellbound; the Guv'nor heard it all as if in a dream.

'I'd like to go there,' said Sebastian at last.

'So you shall,' said the Princess. 'You shall all come and visit me next summer!'

At last it was morning; the river mists rose in a great white wall, ducks quacked, the day-shift took over amongst the Power Station staff, traffic began to rumble, people to stir in the street. It was time for the Princess to return to her mistress. She said goodbye and thank you, over and over again, to everyone except Scratch, the Guv'nor and

Oliver; these three were to escort her to the Ritz.

'See you in the summer!' she said to all the cats, and they chorused in reply, 'Yes, next summer in the mountains!'

The walk to the Ritz was a long one but the Princess moved like a thoroughbred and never tired. There was conversation, but the Guv'nor remembered nothing of it, neither did he take part in it. 'It's his poor head,' sighed the Princess sympathetically, in an aside to Oliver. At last the party reached the Ritz; the Princess thanked her three companions again and again. She kissed Oliver, shook paws with Scratch, took the Guv'nor's limp paw, sighed, flicked her ear and gently dropped it again. 'I do so hope you are soon feeling better!' He stammered something incoherent.

Then she was going up the hotel steps, through the doorway. 'Goodbye! Promise me you'll visit me next summer!' And she was gone.

The three cats drew deep breaths; then turned and began retracing their steps to the Power Station.

'Well,' said Scratch, 'we've rescued her orright. Now, next thing is to catch old Pikey.'

'Yes,' said Oliver. 'Settle accounts with that red-sprouter! Ggrrh!'

'Blue mountains,' said the Guv'nor. 'Blue sky.'

'I suppose Manx Scoop will give us a hand?' said Oliver.

''Course he will. He's a great geezer,' said Scratch. 'And old BRAINS here will plan the strategy, won'tcher, me old Goofer Sahib?'

'Daffodils,' sighed the Guv'nor.

'What's he say?' Oliver asked Scratch.

'Strike me. Sounded like daffodils.'

'Where?'

'There ain't none. He's gone daffy 'isself if you ask me.'

'I hope he's all right. D'you think he's sickening for something?'

'You feelin' O.K., Guv? Didn't hit yer head or anythink, did you?' asked Scratch, putting an affectionate paw round the Guv'nor's shoulders.

'Blue eyes!' replied the Guv'nor, in a faraway voice. 'My whiskers, how blue!'

'Blue whiskers!' said Oliver, laughing. 'What tosh!'

'He's got it bad,' said Scratch. 'I shoulda realized. Dropping all them cups and tripping over his own paws every time he took a step.'

'Oh, he always does.'

'He's got it real bad, my son,' said Scratch.

'Got what?'

'You'll find out some day. You're only a nipper yet,' said Scratch. 'You 'old his arm one side, I'll hang on the other. He don't know where he is, poor geezer.'

'Blue lake. Blue mountains. Clouds. Daffodils,' murmured the Guv'nor. 'Blue. Very blue.'

'It was that funny-tasting tea,' said Oliver. 'Enough to make anyone see blue daffodils!'

But Scratch merely shook his head, as if to say that this one was beyond young Oliver.

11. All on our Way

Whisky Bylines, newspapercat to his whiskertips, wrote up his story of capture by Wilberforce Pike, rescue of the Princess and escape, so brilliantly that not only was it given world-wide syndication but also won him the much-coveted Top-Press-Cat Prize for the year. This was hard luck on Manx Scoop, who himself so very nearly had been the one to get the story; but Manx took Whisky's triumph very generously. 'I've said it before and I will say it again: Bylines isn't my personal cup of cat-mint, but he's a damn good journalist. And that is what counts.'

As a result of Whisky's forceful exposure of the cat-thief the Royal Feline Crime Squad raced, hot-footed, to the Pike home-stead, but it was empty. Wilberforce and his lady had vanished without trace.

The story of the stolen champion Siamese cat appeared too, although in rather different form, in all the human newspapers. Their version of the tale was simply that of a stolen cat who had, four days after her disappearance, been reported found but who, before she could be returned to her mistress by Mr Smithers, the man who claimed to have found her, had walked into the Ritz all by herself, having miraculously tracked down her mistress in the heart of the metropolis. A popular zoologist wrote a long feature in a Sunday newspaper about baffling aspects of animal instinct.

Scotland Yard ('the human fuzz', to quote Manx Scoop), made extensive inquiries about the mysterious Mr Smithers but, like the Royal Feline Crime Squad (R.F.C.S.), drew a total blank.

The Power Station cats, led by the indefatigable Goofer Sahib, as he was now always called, devoted the whole of that long, dark winter to searching for the Pikes, but without any success.

From time to time there arrived letters from Lollia Paulina, asking if they had caught Wilberforce yet, telling delightful anecdotes of winter-sports in the mountains, inquiring tenderly after the health of them all, and always ending with expressions of affection and fervent hopes of seeing them in the North when the summer came.

These letters, addressed to 'Dear Everyone', were read aloud by Albert (whose short visit still showed no signs of coming to an end). But after he had read them they always disappeared.

At last spring came. Lollia Paulina wrote of daffodils.

One sunny morning, when the military ranks of green tulips were starting to unfurl their colours, scarlet, orange and pink, and the cats were amusing themselves by stalking starlings, Oliver saw, to his astonishment, a well-remembered figure come walking, unhurriedly yet purposefully, along the cats' private track through the shrubbery. Oliver recognized at once this large, lean tom with the so-silent tread and the keen all-seeing eyes as his old neighbour, Mr Tyler.

The visitor had recognized Oliver, too. He said, 'So this is where you got to!' He added, to himself, 'Nothing like a good hunch, Watt. Nothing like a good hunch.'

Oliver was so overwhelmed to see Tyler that all he could find to say was, 'Oh Mr Tyler! It's you, Mr Tyler!'

'Have you a cat here named Governor Goofer, otherwise known as Goofer Sahib?'

'He's over there,' gasped Oliver, nodding in the direction of the iris beds where the Goofer, Manx, Scratch and Nosher were discussing plans for spring-time hunting of Wilberforce Pike.

Tyler nodded thanks. 'I'll have a word with you later, Oliver, about getting you back home.' And he strolled across to the iris beds. Sebastian asked Oliver, 'Who's he?'

'He's Mr Tyler and he comes from near my old home,' said Oliver. 'He knows my family, Seb. He'll be able to show me the way back to them!'

Sebastian's eyes filled with tears. 'You won't g-go and leave us?'

Oliver, to his amazement, found himself hesitating. 'I don't know,' he said, with real astonishment in his voice. 'I always thought that, you know, when the time came, if ever the time did come, that I could go back, you know, I'd go running; but now that the time has come . . . I don't know, Seb. I just don't know!'

Within moments the Goofer called the two young cats over to his group.

'I'm told that you already know the Inspector, Oliver,' said the Goofer. Oliver looked blank.

'He won't know me under that handle,' said Tyler. 'Just knows me as an old neighbour.' He turned to Oliver. 'Detective Inspector Watt Tyler of the Royal Feline Crime Squad Special Security Branch. On your trail, youngster.' He grinned; Oliver blinked. He thought of how he had helped rob the Mayor's banquet. Tyler continued, 'I was away from home when you disappeared; your poor people searched for you all over town, offered a reward; goodness knows they tried to find you! When I got back your very good friend the blackbird called on me; said you'd disappeared and since he'd heard there'd been cat-thieves active in the neighbourhood he feared that one of 'em had nabbed you. There's this particular thief we're interested in at Special Security: Pike, Wilberforce Pike. I've been on his trail for months now, since you disappeared; then there was this Princess stolen and Special Security put me on that case. Then the *Courier* reported how she'd been rescued by you Power Station lot; I went to interview the Princess, she confirmed the story and told me, among other interesting things, that you were down here, young Oliver. So now I've found you, and the Princess is back with her mistress; but I still haven't felt the collar of Wilberforce Pike and until he's safe and sound in the cooler there'll be no rest for me of nights.'

'Nor for any of us,' said Goofer.

Oliver said nothing; he was thinking of the blackbird. His very good friend! Well, so the bird had proved, although Oliver had never thought of him in the light of friendship! And the cat decided that when he did get back to his old home the first thing that he would do would be to spend a whole day digging up worms for the blackbird. A friend in need is a friend indeed!

Watt Tyler was speaking again: 'If you Power Station lot are prepared to work alongside the R.F.C.S. on this job we're likely, together, to find Pike much sooner than if we go on looking for him separately.'

There was a rather uncomfortable pause. Then Nosher said,

'Well, Mr Tyler, it's like this. When all's said and done you're a copper and chumming up with coppers never has bin my policy an' never will be, and I don't think it's the policy of none of my mates, neither.'

'None of us lot ever stooped to bein' coppers' narks, yet,' said Scratch.

'Fair enough,' grinned Watt. 'All that I understand. But think it over a bit more, lads, before you turn it down flat.' He cocked an eye at the Goofer. 'What does your Guv'nor feel about it?'

'I look at it this way,' said the Goofer thoughtfully. 'Which is our biggest enemy: the cops, or the old red-sprouter? Which is the worst menace to cats as a whole: the R.F.C.S. or Pike?'

'Pike!' chorused everyone.

'There you are then,' said the Goofer. 'Far as I'm concerned that settles the matter. We go in with Watt Tyler on this job.'

'Fair enough,' said Scratch. 'In with the cops it is, then, for this Pikey lark. But we must be granted full amnesty, Mr Tyler, for any little jobs wot us lot's done in the past and wot you mightn't think too highly of, if you dig?'

'That's very reasonable,' said Tyler. 'I'll agree to that.' He turned to Oliver. 'And now, young shaver, there's the question of getting you back to your lawful owners.' Oliver was looking miserable and confused. He said, 'I don't know. Maybe they won't want me. Maybe I've grown too rough.'

'Nonsense, those good folks will have you back like a shot. Haven't taken another kitten in your stead, or anything like that. A good clean up will soon have you looking respectable again and it's entirely in your own interest to return to them; they'll give you a decent upbringing, good education. Homes of that sort don't grow on trees, you know.'

'I know that, Mr Tyler, but . . .'

'Take a short stroll, kid, and think it over while we give Mr Tyler a catnip,' suggested the Goofer, kindly.

So Oliver went for a stroll and thought, while Watt Tyler and his new accomplices drank catnip. At last Oliver returned, looking very determined, and announced, 'I can't go back yet. I swore that oath, remember? "By my whiskers and the full moon, I shall never rest until Wilberforce Pike is caught and brought to justice!" I shall just have to stay with you lot until we've caught him.'

Scratch patted Oliver proudly. 'That's the spirit, kid! You're a real rye mush!'

Oliver had no idea what a rye mush might be; but whatever it was, Scratch had clearly paid him a great compliment. As for all the other cats, they mewed, 'Good old Oliver! Stick with us kid! Justice for Pikey, or perish together!'

And now the hunt for Wilberforce Pike started up again in real earnest. Watt Tyler had cat detectives posted at every main railway station and bus terminus. Plainclothescats lurked, nightly, on patches of waste-ground, in parks and recreation-grounds, about and between back-yards and gardens; all the places where cats love to prowl at night and cat-thieves prowl also. Goofer Sahib's gang searched all the little back-streets where the Pikes might be expected to have found a new home; they questioned scores and scores of underground contacts, tapped the cat-vine, peered and pried, crept and clambered, looked and listened, never resting. Manx Scoop, using his bachelor-flat in Ebury Street as his H.Q., acted as liaison-officer between the Tyler cats and the Goofer cats. But all to no avail; as Nosher expressed it, Mr and Mrs Pike had hopped the twig good and proper.

Then one morning early in June, when the Power Station cats, weary with searching, were lying on a shed roof sunning them-selves and thinking lazily of nothing in particular, there was a sudden scurry and Manx Scoop stood amongst them, grinning.

'*Saludos amigos!* You have yourselves a truly fine sun-trap here! Forgive me for disturbing you but I have news. Very hot news, requiring action this day.'

Everyone sat up.

'My faithful mongoose, who always does his own marketing, was this morning buying eggs and eels in Pimlico when he happened to glance up and saw a man and woman, exactly resembling the description which you, *amigos*, have so cor-rectly and excellently and often given him of Mr and Mrs Pike. Without a moment's hesitation he hid his shopping-bags behind a Wall's ice-cream sign standing conveniently at hand, and followed Mr and Mrs Pike who, loaded with luggage, hailed a taxi shortly after Ranjit commenced trailing them and drove off in it. My truly distinguished bearer, who is not a Sikh for nothing (a very great race, the Sikhs), at once leapt on to a small horse-drawn lumber-cart that was providentially drawn up, driverless, at the kerbside. Ranjit Singh hissed to the horse to follow the taxi and so away went the horse at full gallop with Ranjit driving; they swerved in and out of the traffic, says Ranjit, like a gun-carriage answering an emergency call up to the lines. A certain amount of lumber fell from the cart and they were chased by a policeman on a scooter who was unseated, although luckily not hurt, by a roll of old carpet which fell from the back of the cart to land in the path of the scooter. Thus, thanks to Ranjit's skilled handling of the reins, the truly splendid co-operation of the horse and a certain degree of good luck, the Pike taxi was followed successfully to Victoria coach station where Ranjit, with little difficulty, dogged the Pikes and saw them take seats on a bus. He heard Wilberforce ask the driver if the bus were going to Ambleside. Therefore we must conclude, *amigos*, that it is to this place, Ambleside, that the Pikes have gone.'

'It's a dead tumble,' said Scratch.

'Ambleside, where's that?' asked Selina.

'This I have checked and it is by a lake in the far North; if I am not mistaken very near, or quite near, that lake by which our Siamese Princess resides,' replied Manx. He paused, lit a Gauloise cigarette. 'Which could be very useful.'

'Them Pikes must be follered, pronto,' said Scratch.

'Exactly.'

'The Lollyp-pop is always asking us to s-stay with her when summer c-comes,' said Sebastian.

'Summer is truly here,' said Manx, blowing smoke rings into the hot blue sky.

'Do we write to her, asking if it will be O.K. for us to come and stay?' asked Oliver.

'Certainly not,' said Albert. 'Most rude.'

'Then what do we do?' inquired Ninette.

'Drop her . . . convey to her – ah, um . . . a tactful hint that . . . er, summer is here,' said Albert.

'But blimey, old mate, she oughter know summer's come without no gentle hints from us!' said Nosher.

'Can't waste time on hints,' said Scratch. 'We need action, fast.'

'Send her a telegram,' said Manx, blowing more rings:

'SALUDOS, PRINCESS! WE ARE ON OUR WAY.'

'Incredibly rude,' said Albert.

'Which of us sends it?' asked Oliver.

'On no account let my name appear on it,' said Albert.

'Goofer Sahib,' said Manx, blowing an extra large ring and watching, with an innocent expression, this large ring float up into the air, growing larger and loopier as it rose higher and higher. 'Goofer Sahib sends it.'

'I refuse to participate,' said Albert. 'Make that clear, Goofer. I refuse to be guilty of such uncivil behaviour.'

Goofer Sahib, nodding his head, went off without a word.

'Does he remember her address?' asked Oliver. 'You know how vague he is.'

'There are times when the vaguest of cats becomes the soul of efficiency,' said Manx, much amused over something that Oliver had missed.

The Goofer soon returned. 'That's been done.'

'Splendid,' said Manx. 'Now we await her reply.'

The reply came in record speed in the form of a telegram addressed to Goofer Sahib. It read, simply: 'LOVELY. LOLLIA P.'

On hearing this all the cats, except Albert, cheered frenziedly.

'Another telegram must now be sent,' said he, in his furriest voice, 'to inform the Princess that I shall not be one of the party.'

'Oh, come on Albert!' mewed everybody.

'No, no; I refuse to invite myself in such a grossly discourteous fashion. Another telegram must be dispatched, Goofer, saying that I am not coming,' repeated Albert.

'No need. I've already told her,' said the Goofer.

'Oh?'

'My telegram to her said, "SALUDOS, PRINCESS! WE ARE ALL ON OUR WAY, EXCEPT ALBERT".'

99

'And she sent back it was lovely!' chortled Nosher.

All the cats rocked with laughter. 'Poor old Albert! Didn't fancy you, mate!'

Albert looked dreadfully glum. 'I shall cut short my visit to this Power Station, Goofer Sahib, and return to my old school-master. I feel that I have grasped the national grid, and that there is little, if anything, left for me to learn further about shedding the load . . .'

'Nonsense,' intervened Manx. 'We can't spare you at this stage, Albert, dear boy. Some cat who is truly intelligent and reliable must remain here at this Power Station as anchor-man while we are all absent and that cat, *amigo*, is yourself.'

'Absolutely,' said the Goofer.

'Can't do without you, old Albert,' said Scratch. 'Got to leave a real good cat this end, and that good cat is you.'

'If Albert's gonna be left here all on his jack, then I'm staying with him,' announced Ninette. 'He can't possibly manage by himself. He'll need someone to cook, and take care of him.'

'I have changed my mind, Goofer Sahib; I shall be happy to stay,' announced Albert, quickly.

So it was decided. Albert was to stay at the Power Station as anchor-man and Ninette was to stay to take care of Albert. The rest of the cats were to go North. Manx Scoop and Ranjit Singh to accompany them.

Manx went to telephone Watt Tyler about these developments in the Pike hunt. The other cats began packing what few things they needed to take with them. Albert strutted around looking very important, and Ninette set about baking him a sparrow-pie to demonstrate how greatly he needed her.

12. In a Summer Palace

The cats travelled northwards all night; Manx driving his own
Land-Rover with Nibs, Twinkey, Crusoe, Oliver, Sebastian and
the mongoose in it. A second Land-Rover, provided by Special
Security and driven by Scratch and the Goofer, turn and turn
about, held Selina, Boney, Nosher, Randy and Sam. This
made a total force of thirteen cats and a mongoose, sufficient
to capture Wilberforce Pike several times over, as Manx said.

At dawn the little convoy found itself driving along a wind-
ing road between stone-walls built long ago, with high
mountains looming out of the lightening sky and processions of
great sleepy clouds swimming over the mountains. As the sun
strengthened more and more chains of mountains unfolded
themselves before the astonished cats, and more and more
clouds, painted pink by the dawn glow, floated in from the
west, where the sea lay.

Presently the cats saw a lake gleaming and curving, with
layers of white mist rising from it and stirring in slow dreamy
shoals away from the lake and up the narrow valleys between
the mountains. Everything was serene, silent, tranquil; the
lower slopes of the mountains were green with young bracken,
the summits were plum-blue with shadow or, where the sun
touched them, shining and rosy.

The Land-Rovers drove past hamlets of little grey and white
cottages, past farms and walled fields where cattle and sheep
grazed. At last they rolled into a small, crooked town and
Manx said it was Ambleside. Here, in some boarding-house,
slumbered the Pikes; not yet awake and certainly not yet
aware of the revengeful cats.

Manx had been recommended to a tiny, but spotlessly clean
cat-café where the travellers refreshed themselves with milk;
for they still had a high pass to cross to reach the lake on whose
shores the Princess lived. Away the Land-Rovers went again;
climbing up and up a long, narrow, windy road into the clouds.

Here the sunshine vanished; a moist and chilly vapour blew thickly over them. All that the cats could see of the scenery was an occasional glimpse of frighteningly steep black mountainsides scattered with giant boulders. Selina said loudly that she didn't like it. 'All them rocks. Why ain't there no nice grass? All them big stones; coo, it's awful!'

And now came a dizzy descent which scared not only Selina but the other cats as well. Goofer Sahib, who was driving, hung on to the wheel, desperately following the narrow, twisting and turning road, which plunged ever downwards into a valley deep as a well, where shone another lake. The Land-Rovers safely reached the lakeside, drove along a road by the tree-fringed shore. Smooth silver reaches of water on which slept tiny islands, rocky bays overhung by massive crags, waterfalls streaking silver between curtains of birch leaves; it was all breathtakingly beautiful. Goofer Sahib's eyes strayed from the road and the Land-Rover almost hit a sheep who was sauntering apparently without any thought of traffic. The sheep bleated indignantly while the Goofer jammed on his brakes, stuck his head out of the Land-Rover and bawled, 'Wanter get run over, you silly old bag?'

A very prim and proper-looking female cat came at that moment through a gap in the hedge; she was carrying a basket of eggs and a bunch of rhubarb. She flung the Goofer a highly disapproving glance. He said, ' 'ere, d'you know where this is?' and handed her a piece of paper with the Princess's address written on it.

The prim cat read the address; she looked more disagreeable than ever. 'It is that house there,' she said, pointing to a big, grey, turreted building that could be glimpsed among trees on their left. 'You will find the drive a few yards farther along the road. The tradesmen's entrance is at the back of the house.' And staring very hard and nastily at the Goofer and then at his passengers she handed him back his piece of paper. 'Thank you for nothing, sourpuss,' said the Goofer, and drove on.

The drive led between rhododendrons thick with pink, purple and white blooms; stunning to the eye. Goofer Sahib's Land-Rover went first, Manx Scoop's vehicle followed. They emerged upon a vast plain of gravel which spread like a parade-ground before the huge house. Selina said, overawed, 'Oo-er! Like it's a real palace!'

'Ain't so big as our ole Power Station,' said Nosher, always chirpy.

'Ooh, look; there's the Princess! Coo, don't she look smashing!' Selina recovered her bounce in her delight at seeing Lollia Paulina, who was standing waiting for them, not on the steps of the mansion, but by a pretty little wooden summer-house among the rhododendrons. All the cats jumped from the Land-Rovers and rushed towards the Princess, who ran to meet them. Now came a general embracing and paw-shaking and mewing and exclaiming; Manx was seen gallantly kissing the Princess's paw. The Goofer, who had driven like an angel through the worst of the country, relapsed into goofishness and before he had even shaken paws with Lollia Paulina had put one leg in a bird-bath and then pulled Nibs into it with him. The Princess, rocking with laughter, helped them out.

'You can't think how lovely it is to see you all again! I was so thrilled when I got your telegram, Goofer dear! I can't tell you!'

The Goofer tried to say something equally warm and friendly, but could think of nothing suitable; he made a queer gulping sound instead, stepped backwards and found himself once more in the bird-bath. Once more he was pulled out.

The Princess who, as Selina had said, looked smashing in an exquisite silk caftan with a jade necklace at her throat and another wound round her tail, now became deliciously hostessy.

'You will all want breakfast and something to eat,' she purred. 'Come this way; you aren't staying in the big house but in my own special apartment in the grotto. I think you will find it more comfortable; not so stiff and formal, and well out of the way of Mrs Cartmel-Coniston-Cartmel-Carr who is always perfectly darling to me, but . . . oh, you know!'

'Won't want thirteen extra cats and a faithful mongoose turfing round her,' said Manx.

'Exactly. Besides, you'd have to be so much on your best

behaviour with her, while here you can come and go as you please, do as you like; in fact treat it *exactly* as your own home.' The Princess, as she spoke, led the way up the steps of a rockery smothered in blue gentians, snow-in-summer, rock-roses yellow and cerise, purple dianthus; mosses, foxgloves and swaying flax-flowers. The sunny air smelled of thyme and honey.

They reached the top of the steps. 'Welcome to my summer palace!' said the Princess.

She drew aside curtains of green fern-fronds, revealing a cool cave with moss divans, green slate tables, enchanting little chairs and benches; grotto mirrors, silver slivers of looking-glass gleaming on the walls, reflecting here a blue eye, there a black ear, a tail-tip, a quiver of silk caftan. She led her guests from one cave to the next; couches and beds, a music-room with a dulcimer, a great urn full of lilies, a fountain, water droplets falling in lute-plucking cadences. Her visitors had never in their lives seen or dreamt of anything like this; even Manx was overcome. Ranjit Singh muttered something about the Taj Mahal.

'Coo, fancy living 'ere!' gasped Selina over and over again. 'Cor, wouldn't I like it, just!'

'You think you will be happy here?' crooned the Princess.

'Smashin', ab-ser-lootely smashin'!' responded Selina.

They were given breakfast; frogs' legs in cowslip wine, scrambled eggs with cream, cheese patties, mouse *vol-au-vent*. The Princess fussed round them, serving them herself. Ranjit Singh poured the coffee.

'More scrambled egg, Crusoe? What about you, Nibs: another patty? Manx, surely you can manage one more *vol-au-vent*? Selina dear, do help yourself to whatever you fancy. Boney, try these frogs' legs, they really are delicious although I say so myself!'

'Did you cook them, Princess?'

'No, my housekeeper, Mrs Tryphena, did. She is a wonderful cook.'

Boney tried the frogs' legs and pronounced them, 'Bloomin' good, mate.'

'You try some, Goofer Sahib,' said the Princess.

'No thanks, Princess.'

'But you aren't eating *anything*!'

'I'm doing fine, Princess,' said Goofer Sahib, who had totally lost his appetite.

'I do wish you'd call me Lollypop, like you did in your telegram. I'm sure you all do when I'm not there, and it is so sweet.'

There was a stunned silence.

'Lollyp-pop? In my telegram?' blurted the Goofer, wild-eyed.

'Yes.' She put her hand in her caftan and produced the telegram, folded small. She opened it and read, smiling enchantingly: 'SALUDOS, LOLLYPOP. WE ARE ALL ON OUR WAY. EXCEPT ALBERT. DEVOTEDLY, GOOFER.'

Cheers of laughter echoed round the grotto. The Goofer mumbled, 'Slip of the tongue. You can't trust the Post Office to get anything right these days,' he added.

The Princess said nothing, but, flicking her ear, folded the telegram very carefully and put it back in her pocket.

At this point there entered the cave the sour-faced female whom they had met in the lane. The Princess took her by the arm. 'Mrs Tryphena, let me introduce you to my friends from the South. Everyone; my good friend and housekeeper, Mrs Tryphena! Tryphena, this is Goofer Sahib, whom you have heard so much about, and Mr Scoop, and Miss Selina . . .' And so one by one the cats were introduced; Mrs Tryphena looking very pinch-faced as she shook paws: 'How nice to meet you! Delighted!' she murmured, unconvincingly.

After breakfast the travel-wearied cats rested in the garden. Later, however, after a light luncheon of minnows-on-toast, they decided that pleasure must no longer delay the object of their visit. 'Must make a recce in Ambleside, Princess,' said Manx.

'Oh, do let me come too!'

'Rather you didn't, this time,' said Manx, politely. 'We want, on this trip, to be as little noticed as possible and, if you will permit me to say so, nobody on this good earth could ever fail to notice you. Eh, Goofer Sahib?'

'What?'

'The Princess wants to come with us, but I'm telling her she's much too much of an eye-catcher to take on a quiet recce.'

'I'll remove all my jewellery!' offered the Princess, eagerly.

'It's not really the jewellery that one . . . er . . . notices,' said the Goofer.

'Oh, can't I come? Please! I do so love an adventure!'

'If old Pike sees you he'll remember you for sure and then p'raps he'll recognize us, and then the game wil be U-P, up, before it's even begun. You stay here, Princess,' said the Goofer firmly. The Princess pouted, 'Oh, you are horrid!'

At which Goofer Sahib stumbled away, followed by the privately smiling Manx.

'I shall have to go back to the Smoke,' said Goofer, miserably. 'There's something about me annoys her. You'll have to take over, Manx.'

'Oh, nonsense. What she needs, like all females, is firm handling. You spoke to her precisely in the right tone. Never let a bird get the upper hand, even a Princess bird,' said Manx. 'You're doing fine. Come on, let's get out those Land-Rovers.'

In Ambleside Mr and Mrs Pike were strolling quietly through the town. Mrs Pike remarked upon the large number of cats. 'Seem to be everywhere.'

'Yus,' replied Wilberforce, 'real good town for cats, this is. Real good town. In fact, I'm beginnin' to regret being on 'oliday. Vexes me to see all them good cats going to waste.'

They walked a little farther up the street. There were cats on every doorstep, cats seated on all the walls, cats crouched under bushes, cats up trees, cats pacing along pavements, cats peering round the corners. And all were watching the Pikes with big unblinking eyes.

'Gets on your nerves; so many cats as this,' said Mrs Pike uneasily.

'If it weren't for the money in 'em I'd give up cats,' said Wilberforce. 'Try me hand with tropical fish. Breed and sell what-d'ye-call-'ems. Nice and silent, fish is. Don't scratch neither.'

Mrs Pike suddenly seized her husband's arm. 'Look! That 'at there; ain't he young Gospo?'

'One white cat is very like another.'

'I'm *sure* it's young Gospo! Know that cat anywhere, I would.'

'It's certainly very like him. Still, one white cat is very . . .'

'An' that cat grinning with all them teeth; I'm sure I seen him before! And that kitten there . . . look, 'im! And 'er! Oh Pikey, I don't like it! I think they're after us!'

'After us! Don't be daft!'

'I don't like it!' repeated Mrs Pike. And she made Wilber-force hurry back with her to their boarding-house. The cats followed. Having run their quarry to earth they posted a guard, Nosher and Nibs, at the boarding-house gate and sent a telegram to Watt Tyler. Then, feeling that this was a good day's work, the cats returned to the Princess and dinner at the summer palace.

13. 'Music Hath Charms'

Watt Tyler, hurrying out of R.F.C.S. headquarters after a top-level security conference following the arrival of the telegram from Ambleside, found himself button-holed by Whisky Bylines; a cat who was a constant nuisance to him.

'Any news, Inspector? Anything heard yet, of the Pikes? Is it true that you've had a message from Guv'nor Goofer?'

'No comment; no comment,' rasped Watt Tyler, shoving past the reporter.

'There's a very strong rumour going the rounds that Guv'nor Goofer has caught the Pikes.'

'First I've heard of it.'

'One more question, Inspector. Do you think . . .'

'Never!' snapped Watt, diving headlong into a squad car that was waiting for him. The car drove off.

Whisky, without ado, stopped a taxi and told the driver to take him to the Power Station. He knew that Albert was there, holding the fort and without doubt being kept in touch with news from Ambleside.

Albert and Ninette were having a cosy after-dinner game of poker, amongst the water-pipes beneath the General's tail, or rather what now remained of the tail: the red bow only being recognizable. Albert was armed with his rusty old rifle; Ninette was wearing a pair of snappy blue high socks on each hind leg and in each sock was tucked a sheath-knife. Whisky decided that in this case the female was certainly the deadlier of the species.

'Hello. Without beating about the bush, any news from Ambleside?'

'Don't know anyone in Ambleside,' replied Albert.

'My dear chap, kid me not. The entire newspaper world from *Kit-Bits Weekly* to the *Mousing Evening Comet* knows that Manx Scoop, bless his heart, and all the Power Station gang, bar yourself and this enchanting little lady here, are racing

ound Ambleside on a hot tip that there they will discover the
Pikes.' Whisky paused and cleared his throat. 'Furthermore,
now have an even hotter tip that Guv'nor Goofer and gang
have found the Pikes and that Wilberforce is about to meet a
very sticky fate.'

'Really!' gasped Albert. 'That's marvellous news!'

'You hadn't heard?'

'We've heard nothing.'

'Then I'm telling you now.'

'Very kind of you,' said Ninette sarcastically.

There was a loud scuttling sound. Whisky jumped. 'What's
hat?'

'One of the General's rats, I shouldn't be surprised,' said
Albert. 'Since we've been on our own here they've grown very
bold again. To tell you the truth, Ninette and I are expecting
a raid any time; we rather think they'll try to get back the
General's tail.'

Whisky suddenly remembered that he had to hurry away.

But, as it turned out, Albert did not need his rifle, nor
Ninette the knives inside her stockings.

The rat who had overheard Whisky's conversation with
Albert had naturally taken the news straight back to Sergeant
Fleaby and Fleaby had at once gone to the General.

'Sticky fate for Wilberforce, eh?' said the General. 'Old
Pike in a tight corner, is 'e?' He resumed chewing, very
houghtfully, the rubber ring that he had sneaked from under
a baby's pram in a back-garden. At length he spoke again.
'Ow long it take us rats to get up there d'you think, Sergeant?'

'Get up where, sir?'

'Lake Country, in the North.'

'Good three weeks' march, sir.'

'Too long. Them cats will 'ave settled Pike's 'ash afore that.'

'You goin' to Pike's rescue, sir?'

'Pike's the henemy o'cats. Cats is henemies of rats. Anyone
wot's the henemy of cats is a hally of rats. Stands ter reason,
Serg.'

'Yus, s'pose it do, sir.'

'It do an' all, Sergeant.'

'Then we go campaigning North, sir?'

' 'S right. You'll 'ave to arrange transport, Sergeant. Take too long to march. Think modern, Sergeant.'

'Very good, sir.'

'Soon as you can make it, Sergeant.'

'Yessir.'

'See the troops is hinformed.'

'Yessir.' The Sergeant stood lopsidedly to attention, saluted and scuttled out.

He was speedily back.

'Transport all harranged, sir.'

The General, still busy with the rubber ring, looked up with his mouth full.

'There's a furniture-van we can all stow away on, sir. Bound for a place called Barrer. Goes through Kendal, which is very near this 'ere Hamboneside. Van leaves at heighteen 'ours prompt, sir, from back o' the furniture store.'

The General swallowed his mouthful of chewed rubber.

'Well done, Sergeant. See all your men is on board well on time, in battle-dress, fully armed.'

'Yessir.'

The rats arrived at Kendal next morning at crack of dawn, spilling out of the furniture-van while the driver, who had been quite unaware that he carried passengers, let alone a full regiment bound for active service, went into an all-night café for breakfast. Sergeant Fleaby quickly found his troops rations in the form of an enormous bin stacked with tourist-litter; after a goo   feed the rats rested an hour, then formed a column and beg   the march to the town they called Hamboneside.

Full daylight   lted them before they were half-way there; they lay up all day in a deserted hen-house. At nightfall they started off again and were in Hamboneside, garrisoned in a derelict outhouse, by the next sunrise.

Contact was made with the local rats, who gave prompt information about the invasion by a gang of foreign cats. The rats also knew all about the Pikes. 'The cats follow them everywhere they gar, seesta. And now a new chap's arrived on scene, like; cat-detective they say, like.'

The local rats agreed to join forces with the General's rats to turn the Power Station cats out of Hamboneside. 'This was a quiet town once; unspoilt, verra nice spot, like. We don't want it overrun with offcome cats, don't want that at all.'

Watt Tyler had set up his H.Q. at Troutbeck. The Ambleside and Troutbeck cats, alerted about Wilberforce Pike, were perfectly willing (indeed, caterwauling-keen, as Manx Scoop expressed it in one of his dispatches to the *Times*) to join in the attempt to capture the cat-thief and bring him to justice.

The problem was, how to do it? Mr and Mrs Pike seemed to suspect that they were in danger; the large number of cats in Ambleside struck them as odd, even more singular was the fact that some of these cats seemed recognizable as animals who had at one time been prisoners of theirs and who had escaped. Gospo, as they called Oliver, was particularly a case in point.

The Pikes, therefore, only ventured out when there were other humans around; they took good care to frequent places teeming with tourists. They favoured coach day-trips; a six-lakes tour, trips to Grasmere, to Morecambe, to Keswick, to Coniston and Hawkshead. Solitude they avoided like the plague.

Watt Tyler, learning of the arrival of the rats, went straight to the Power Station cats with this news. 'This is serious. Means real danger. They've linked up with the local boyos and that makes quite a large army. And they're out to get us.'

'Can't we rustle up a large force of local cats?'

'Not so easy. These high country cats are mountaineer types; live in scattered farms, aren't even domesticated most of 'em; they're as good as wild cats, almost impossible to contact. Aren't even on the cat-vine, most of 'em. Those I've been able to get interested are keen enough; but we still can't match the rats in number; nowhere near.'

'Difficult,' said Manx. 'Very.'

'Take too long to fetch in squadrons of town cats from Northern cities, I s'pose?' said Goofer Sahib.

'Far too long. Old Pike won't linger that length of time. He's already got the wind up. We got to nab him quick, or he'll be gone.'

'What about our local terriers?' suggested the Princess.

'Dogs!' spat all the cats.

'Dogs, I agree, are not a cat's favourite animal, but these are working terriers and will take on all manner of jobs and be really very obliging, so long as one repays them with bones and biscuits and so forth.'

'What kind of work will they do?' asked Scratch.

'Well, most of them work for the hunt during the winter months, and in summer they act as mountain guides. But they'll dig holes, deliver long-distance messages, and many of them are splendid rat-catchers.'

'Terriers do make first-rate ratters,' agreed Watt. 'Are they expensive to hire?'

'They're not cheap, but they are well worth what they charge,' said the Princess.

'How do we contact them?'

'You had best send a message to Newlands, asking Wee Hamish McCall to come over with a strong party of rat-catchers to deal with a plague of rats. A *large* plague of rats; then he'll bring plenty of terriers. There's a trail-hound neighbour of mine going Lorton way this afternoon; he'll see that the message is passed to Wee Hamish, I'm certain. I'll tip him a few chocolate biscuits; he'd sell his soul for chocolate biscuits.'

The trail-hound proved helpful, the message was passed to Newlands. At midday next day a party of terriers was seen trotting up the driveway and skipping over the rockery to present themselves at Lollia Paulina's summer palace, where Watt Tyler and the other cats were waiting to meet them.

Their leader was a gay-looking little terrier, rather shaggy and with a collection of bits of dried heather and old leaves sticking to him; he sported a Highland bonnet, a well-worn plaid and carried bagpipes under his arm. This was the famous Wee Hamish McCall. 'His mother was named Fifi, which is French,' Lollia Paulina had explained, 'and his father was a rather mysterious West Highlander whom Fifi met in Edinburgh; all very romantic and resulting in Wee Hamish, who ultimately crossed the Border and settled here. He's a great personality, very colourful, as you'll soon discover!'

Wee Hamish came bounding up the rockery, pulled aside the fern-curtains and poked in his head. Then he made a face and muttered over his shoulder to somebody behind him, 'Och, what a terrible pong o' cats!' Then he popped his head in again and barked, 'Princess! Princess!'

The Princess moved forward gracefully. 'Good afternoon, Hamish. Do come in.'

In bustled Hamish, accompanied by a medley of terriers, some rough-haired and tousled, some smooth-haired; all muddy, all plainly very tough. Hamish introduced them: Brat Wilson the Lakeland terrier; Rabsie, an Aberdeen; Pooks, a Sealyham; old Alec the Border terrier; Titch and Tiny, fox-terriers who always travelled on a coupling-chain; Jack Russell, wee and wiry; Sankey and Moody, Skye terriers, Sankey with second-sight; Yorky Boy; Bits, hairy as a beatnik. They clustered round, yapping dementedly.

'Are you all ratters?' asked Watt Tyler, when at last he could make himself heard.

'Och aye,' said Hamish. 'Aye, aye,' yapped his companions.

'All used to fighting?' queried Watt. Oliver, staring open-mouthed at this collection of wild ones from the hills, thought there was no need to ask that particular question. The terriers grinned happily and wagged their stumpy little tails. 'Aye.'

'Willing to take on a large army of rats?'

'Ohaye!' they all said.

'It may be a bit of a ticklish do,' said Goofer Sahib. 'That won't worry you, I suppose?'

'Nay, nay,' said Wee Hamish. 'Just how we like it.'

So it was agreed that the terriers should join forces with the cats against the rats. Payment was quickly decided upon; a large sack of dog biscuits to be shared amongst them and a sheep's head each.

The terriers' plan was a surprise attack on the rats in their garrison, but reconnaissance quickly revealed that the wily General had anticipated this and had lodged his troops in scattered billets throughout Hamboneside and in nearby farms, cottages and hen-houses.

'He's a canny wee fella, knows what he's up to, yon General,' sighed Wee Hamish. 'What size is he?'

'Large for a rat, very,' said Goofer Sahib. 'Almost the size of Titch, there.'

'Jings!' said Hamish with a long whistle.

'Gay plenty to get tha teeth into,' grinned Brat Wilson.

The question, as usual, was how to tempt the rats out to fight in the open.

'They must come out in t'open, like,' explained Alec. 'You cats stalk and catch rats in some verra narrow places, like, but us terriers need 'em to come right out, like, into rick-yard, like, or shippen floor, like; we need room.'

'Trouble with rats,' said Jack Russell, 'is that they don't like fighting. That is, they'll never come out looking for a fight, like, as a terrier will. Corner a rat, and of course he'll fight like a demon; but only because he has to. When rats do attack they like to do it in large numbers; and so, when they come, we need to ambush 'em; surprise 'em in some place where we can pounce on them all together and *dee-mol-ish* 'em.' (He dwelt on the word lovingly.)

'I weel mind when yan rat army gar ower frae Lantit Green,' said Titch. 'Nigh on hundred of 'em, I doubt, gar ower Gaskitt Gill ah set for Braitit. Ahr lads hid waitin' for 'em in t'owd borran in yon narrer place under crags and dropped on 'em as they gar ayant trod there and chopped 'em doon. By gum! our jaws ached wi' choppin'!'

The terriers greeted this with roars of laughter. Lollia Paulina also laughed; she understood the dialect. But the other cats barely comprehended a word; although, equally, the terriers found the cats very strange spoken.

'Oh, we must plan how to tempt out a really *huge* rat army!' exclaimed the Princess, clapping her paws at the thought. 'A really lovely enormous army of them!'

'Let's hope you find 'em as much fun when the time comes!' grinned Scratch.

The terriers listened to this with their heads cocked on one side and their noses twitching.

That night there was a full moon and the Princess held a ball in the garden, with dancing on the lawns to a three-piece orchestra of cat's saxophone, ukelele and double-bass, with Twinkey joining in with his piano-accordion. Wee Hamish adding the bagpipes and Pooks on the drums. Sankey and

Moody sang. There were catnip and champagne to drink and a buffet of cold chicken, crayfish in parsnip-wine, snail-and-bacon pie, cow'd leady (a local dish, for the terriers), cheese-fritters and sponge-cake. Selina, much cleaned-up, her freshly shampooed hair dressed with flowers, and wearing one of Lollia Paulina's silk caftans and pearls, looked so very different from her usual self, indeed such an eyeful, that she made conquests right and left. Lollia Paulina was glamorous beyond words in floating chiffon and a diamond tiara.

So the dancing, feasting and merrymaking went on all night. In the small hours, when moonlight had waned and the landscape was darkening, the Princess, abandoning herself to an urge for solitude (she was a creature of caprice), went to walk alone by the lake. The broad pearl-grey waters merged into a paler mist, ripples sadly and gently lapped the shore, the birches rustled in the wind of coming dawn. The Princess, always poetic, seated herself on a rock and stared pensively at the lake.

The long ripples linked themselves one to the other in strands and bars of dark on light; moving and quivering, always advancing to the shore, each pattern of ripples replaced without pause by new ripples, so that ripples were always where they had always been. The lake, in this manner, was eternally stealing shorewards and eternally lying where it had for ever lain. Dreamily watching the lake thus for ever creeping shorewards the Princess sat for some time before she noticed that the ripples seemed to be running farther up the shore than usual, so that the very ground itself appeared to be moving. Intrigued, she stood up and peered intently; then she uttered a series of shrill, panic-stricken cries. The shore was alive with rats, swimming in from the lake; hundreds upon hundreds of them for ever swimming in and swimming in, crawling out of the water and up the dry ground between the boulders and the trees.

Lollia Paulina's cries halted the rats for a moment; they raised their heads, sniffing the air and testing it with their whiskers. Too terrified now to move or utter another cry she stood like an image on her rock, frozen in the knowledge that if they scented her the rats would have her torn to shreds in an instant. Then a large bulk soared through the air; there was a rustle of squeaks from the rats below, 'An owl! An owl! Air-attack! Take cover!' A myriad feet scuttled for bushes, as though a stream of water suddenly swirled about the Princess on her rock. The bulky flying object landed beside her; it was Goofer Sahib. She flung herself into his arms. 'Rats! Thousands of rats!'

From the water's edge came Sergeant Fleaby's hoarse voice, 'Wot'sa matter? Why dontcher keep movin', troops up in front there? Keep movin', I tell yer; keep the landin'-beach clear!'

'Air-attack, Serg!'

'Hair-attack! I'll give yer perishin' hair-attack! Your horders is to keep movin', up to the 'ouse!'

The Princess and Goofer Sahib watched as the rats scattered from under the bushes back to open ground; they now lost their bearings, for a moment at least, and squirmed in circles, squeaking, 'Which way? Which way?'

In the garden, beyond the trees, the orchestra started up again; a lively reel, led by the pipes of Wee Hamish. The General's shrill voice rang out in command to his rat battalions, 'Follow the music!'

The rats wheeled round as one and began pouring up the high lakeside banks towards the sound of the orchestra. Goofer Sahib gasped, 'No time to waste!' picked up the Princess and, clutching her closely, took a prodigious leap for the bushes to the right of the rat column. He and his burden landed in a heap; the Princess exclaimed, 'I've lost my tiara!'

'No time to worry about that now; c'mon Lollypop!' And Goofer hauled her to her feet and raced for the house, dragging the Princess after him.

Dementedly he and his companion burst amongst the care-free, whirling dancers. 'Quick! Rats! Thousands of 'em! Get marching, Hamish, and keep playing! Their order is follow the music! Let 'em follow it to the best ambush you can think of! Hurry!'

'Mosed'le Beck lads, ambush in Mosed'le Beck!' yapped Wee Hamish to the terriers. Then he turned sharply on his heel and went piping away through Flencoyne Wood, with Pooks drumming beside him. The terriers fell in behind and all the cats and Ranjit Singh, the mongoose, fell in behind the terriers. The double-bass player flung aside his heavy instrument and joined the other cats; Twinkey, too, dropped his piano-accordion and ran to march with his pals. The saxophonist followed Twinkey, but kept tight clutch on his saxophone.

Terriers and cats climbed hurriedly up the mossy slopes between the trees, behind the music of Hamish and Pooks. They emerged on open ground above the wood, where a small beck ran down a steep, narrow valley. Here Hamish halted, though he never stopped piping, and the other animals halted also. Alec hastily posted them above and behind two great boulders on either side of the track and here they waited breathlessly while Wee Hamish skirled out 'The Gay Gordons' and Pooks beat a stirring rhythm. Alec snapped a last command, 'Take the officers prisoner, kill the rest.'

There was not long to wait. Soon a deep rustling was heard, like wind in a forest, and the banks of the beck grew black and began to quiver. Nearer and nearer came the rats and now the moving ground was pricked with a thousand spots of fire which shone closer and closer. Now they were near enough for Oliver to see the General at their head, wearing his cocked hat and carrying a drawn sword which glinted coldly. This Oliver noticed, and he noticed too how the rat battalions closed ranks into a solid mass to pass between the narrowness of the boulders. Then Alec and Goofer Sahib together uttered a whispered, 'Now!' and the waiting ambush fell upon the rats.

There were few prisoners. Goofer Sahib and Oliver both had made for the General and held him between them. Scratch captured the Sergeant. There was a colonel in command of the local rats; he was taken prisoner by Lollia Paulina and Manx. A fearful struggle to secure a fourth prisoner was going on a short distance from the ambush place; there was much furious spitting and hissing and what looked like a ball of interlocked cats and terriers and a bit of brown fur that belonged to no one in particular, but made a loud noise like a kettle boiling over, went rolling over and over down the steep fellside. At last, it rolled to a standstill and sorted itself out; Titch and Tiny and two local cats with the bit of brown fur biting, kicking and struggling between them.

Cats and terriers began hauling the bit of fur up the track towards Alec and Goofer; 'Here's a terrible great rat; eh, by gum, a most serious solid rat . . .' gasped Titch.

'Rat!' shrilled the fur, twisting and writhing like a maniac. 'He who calls me rat . . .!'

'Never seen sich teeth on a rat!' panted the cats.

'R-rr-at! R-rr-at! Such an insult will meet with death by little pieces! I swear by the giant cobra that my great-aunt Messua killed that . . .'

'He must be Field-Marshall at least, by sound of him!' said Tiny.

Manx was trying hard not to laugh.

'May I have this prisoner?' he asked.

'You're welcome,' panted Titch. 'But I warn ye, he bites like a badger.'

Manx stepped forward and the piece of fur simultaneously leapt at Manx. 'Scoop Sahib, I demand the right of reprisal! This insult is too great for less. They have named me rat, and rat again, and yet a third time rat! I demand the right to fight each of these four singly, one by one, and then we shall see who is rat!'

'Ranjit Singh, they will apologize. It was, have no doubt, an error,' said Manx soothingly.

'Aye, it was that,' said Titch, hastily.

The local cats joined in. 'Aye, in t'dark yon l'al creature is verra like a rat.'

Ranjit Singh shrieked and leapt all four feet in the air at once in his rage. 'Rat, again!'

'Ranjit, you are a Sikh and a warrior. We are in the middle of an action and you are holding up that action. Such is not the behaviour of a Sikh. So let us have no more of it; your big insult can be dealt with after we have done what is to be done with these prisoners,' said Manx. He turned to Alec, Watt Tyler and Goofer Sahib, who were earnestly discussing something. 'What *is* to be done with the prisoners?' asked Manx.

'They are to be kept in a strong safe place, under guard,' said Goofer Sahib. 'Alec knows a good place.'

'Aye,' said Alec. 'Waiting-room of owd railway station at Troutbeck. There's hardly any trains stop there nowadays; it's gay quiet.'

And so the prisoners were marched the long march to Troutbeck, across rolling fells and windswept common.

Dawn was fully breaking when the animals reached the deserted-looking station. Hamish tried the waiting-room door. 'It's a grand place, this; there's never any passengers to wait in it and a' they use it for is a Sunday-school.'

The door was unlocked. Hamish led the way in. There was an ancient black fireplace, a wooden bench and an old harmonium. 'Just the job!'

'Job for what?'

'To put the prisoners in!'

The lid of the harmonium was opened without more ado and the General, the Sergeant and the Colonel were thrust inside it. The lid was then closed. Peculiar wheezing, groaning sounds came from within. 'It's them three moving about, seesta,' said Pooks. 'They hit chords, like.'

'Reminds me of Albert,' whispered Sebastian to Oliver. 'Knows the l-lot.'

Sankey, Moody, Crusoe and Boney were left as guard, to do duty in pairs, turn and turn about. The other animals then marched back to Lollia Paulina's palace. They were all very tired but most pleased with themselves; Wee Hamish piped them on their final lap up the drive, with Pooks busy at his drums once more. The saxophonist alone was not happy; he had broken his sax knocking rats on the head with it.

14. Horrible End of Wilberforce Pike

Tired as the animals were, they could not rest for long; there was still Wilberforce Pike to be attended to. So, after some dandelion-coffee, hot rolls and butter and devilled trout, Manx and Watt Tyler, with Oliver and Sebastian as *aides*, drove in a Land-Rover over the pass to Ambleside. They parked on the outskirts of the little town and made their way on foot, unobtrusively, towards the Pike's boarding-house. But as they walked down a quiet side-turning, a big, fat woman and a small skinny one came out of a hotel and Sebastian, after one glance at them, rushed towards the fat one, mewing rapturously: 'It's Miss Pringle! My Miss P-Pringle!'

The fat woman stopped and uttered a cry. 'It's Sebby! It's my little Sebby! Sebby, Sebby, Sebby!'

There was Sebastian rubbing himself against Miss Pringle's legs and purring, and Miss Pringle snatching him up and kissing him and saying, 'My little Seb! Mamma's precious little twiddlums! And didums get lost, den! Did my Sebby find his Mummy, den!' Then, to her companion, 'Fancy finding him here! Hundreds of miles from home! How ever did he get here?'

Sebastian was trying to explain something to Miss Pringle.

'We must keep well out of her way; she's the sort who'll take pity on us and decide to adopt us and give us a good home,' said Goofer Sahib hastily. 'A good home is one thing I could not stand.'

'Nor I,' mewed Watt Tyler.

And Goofer, Watt and Oliver vanished swiftly round a corner. Presently there was a pattering of paws and Sebastian came chasing after them. 'Wait for me!'

'Thought you'd gone back to your Miss Pringle!' sniffed Goofer Sahib.

'I've t-told her all about you, how you're my f-friends and all that, and she says that if you're nice cats then I c-can p-play

with you while she g-goes for a walk. But I've g-got to be
-back for bed-time.'

'Whew!' said Goofer. 'Peter Pan in person, aren't you?'

'I like my Miss P-Pringle,' said Sebastian. 'I'm g-glad I've
ound her again. Ever so g-glad.'

'Fair enough, if you'd rather be with her,' said Goofer
Sahib. 'Don't let me stop you.'

'I'd rather be with you b-both, actually.'

'He's Miss Pringle's cat,' said Watt Tyler. 'Have to be
returned to her anyway, by law, once she was traced. Person-
ally I'm always delighted to see any young cat happy with a
good owner. So let's celebrate Sebastian's reunion with his
Miss Whatsername by getting old Pike's collar felt. C'm
on.'

Near the Pikes' boarding-house they met an excited Nibs
and Nosher.

'The Pikes've gone to Patterdale. On a coach.'

'Patterdale?' repeated Goofer Sahib. That was near where
the Princess lived.

'Yeah. Gonna climb Helvellyn. Least, old Pikey is. Don't
know 'bout his missus. She wants to go 'ome. But the ole red-
sprouter says he's gonna climb Helvellyn before he goes
back.'

'Better get over to Patterdale, but fast,' said Watt. 'We've
got to capture Pike this day!'

The six cats hurried to the Land-Rover. Soon they were in
Patterdale; a cat at the Youth Hostel pointed out the way to
Helvellyn. 'Turn up Grisedale Beck at the bridge. There's a
signpost; you can't miss the way.'

At the signpost Sebastian and Oliver, Nibs, Nosher and
Watt Tyler were dropped off to tail the Pikes, while Goofer
Sahib drove to the palace to call the other animals to the
scene of action: 'CAPTURE PIKE THIS DAY!'

Watt Tyler and his companions hastened along the footpath
leading to the lower slopes of Helvellyn. There was no sign of
the Pikes. The cats came to a car-park near another bridge;
beyond the bridge rose a vast mountainside with a rough
track snaking steeply up it. Several people were slowly plodding up this track; some looking like climbers, others looking

just the reverse. Halfway up went Wilberforce, with Mrs Pike a good way behind him. The cats sped after them.

It was a hot day and the dusty track was gruelling. The cats, not used to mountains, panted for breath. But still they kept on and upwards, until at length they drew level with Mrs Pike. Her tight skirt and her sandal-shoes were totally unsuitable for this kind of walk; her face was purple with struggle. She kept stopping to rest, staring round her as if wondering how on earth she had got to such a terrible place. It was when she stopped like this and turned to look back down the track that she saw the cats.

She screamed. 'Pikey!'

But Wilberforce was too busy sweating upwards to hear her. She screamed again. 'Cats!' Then she noticed Oliver. 'My stars, it's that young Gospo agin! Pikey! Help! They're out to get us!'

Still Pike plodded on, not hearing. Mrs Pike, pallid with terror now, moaned, 'I'm leavin'! Keep yer mountains, keep yer cats; I'm leavin'!' And she began jolting back down the track, moaning to herself as she went, 'Keep yer mountains! I'm leavin'! Just spare me from cats!'

'Nibs, Nosher, follow her!' ordered Watt. Nibs and Nosher spun round and hurried down after Mrs Pike. She staggered to the car-park, waylaid a driver about to leave. 'Take me to the trains, mister, pleasel'

'The only railway-station I shall go near is Troutbeck. I don't know whether that'll be much use to you.'

'That'll do! Anything will do!' gasped Mrs Pike. She tumbled into the car. Nibs and Nosher leapt into the boot. Off they went.

After a longish drive the car stopped, Mrs Pike got out, uttering thanks, the cats got out too. Mrs Pike limped into a funny little building: WAITING-ROOM. Nibs and Nosher peered in through the window. Mrs Pike was huddled on a stool by an old harmonium. She leaned against the keyboard with her eyes closed. There was a very long wait.

At last the lady opened her eyes, sat up straight, became very fidgety. 'Is this train never coming?' She tapped her foot, chewed a hang-nail, stood up, sat down again, idly raised the harmonium-lid to peer inside. Out shot three vast rats. Mrs Pike shrieked, dropped the lid and burst out of the waiting-room as though she had been fired from a gun. A train was approaching; it slowed at the station for the guard to throw out a parcel. Mrs Pike, agile with fright, flung herself aboard the train and vanished in the direction of the Border.

Nibs and Nosher forgot to follow her in their excitement of pouncing on the three rats. Thus, Mrs Pike disappeared, for good and all.

Meanwhile, Wilberforce was still toiling up Helvellyn, followed now by all the cats and the terriers.

The track had grown rougher and rougher, steeper and steeper. The day had become overcast and stuffy with thunder. Many of the people who had first started out on the climb had now turned back, alarmed by the threat of a storm. Yet Wilberforce kept slowly but steadily on, gasping for breath and purple, as if he would explode, the sweat glistening in drops all over his naked dome of head. He had removed his jacket, carried it over his arm. He rolled up his shirt sleeves, then unbuttoned the shirt to his waist, revealing a chest thick with red hair and a white bolster of spare tyre. 'What a very nasty person!' said Lollia Paulina. 'He smells, too. He smells stronger than a fox.'

At last he reached a gap in a stone-wall. Here the fellside ended and the mountain proper began; a chaos of rock and scree. Two long, savagely sharp ridges curved to form a horse-shoe, at the centre of which loomed the massive bulk of the summit. Below the summit, in a deep plunge of basin-shaped hollow, brooded a black tarn. Over all planed a pair of ravens. It was a wild scene.

Wilberforce sat down and mopped his face, neck and bald head with a dirty handkerchief. The animals hid, crouching behind rocks. Now, without talking about it, they all knew exactly what they were going to do.

At last Wilberforce resumed his climb. His route lay along one of the savage ridges. The track followed the apex of the ridge and was very exposed; Wilberforce clearly did not much relish it. On either side of him the mountain fell away in tremendous depths; dizzy to look down. So Wilberforce went very slowly, often holding on to the rock with his hands, going on all fours, or shoving along on his bottom. By the summit cairn two or three people stood; tiny, remote specks. Upon the ridge itself, however, Wilberforce was now the only struggler. And he wondered, as he scrambled, crawled and sweated, why they called this Striding Edge, for he could no more have strode along it than he could have flown over it like a raven.*

Then, as he reached a very nasty place indeed, the path tilted out over space and with slippery little stones sliding under him and bare slippery rock to cling on to, he suddenly saw the cats for the first time. They showed themselves to him, dozens of cats; stared at him, then vanished again. Next time he saw them they were all much nearer and their eyes much rounder and greener. They stared, crouched low; watching him. Then they all disappeared again.

He knew now that they were stalking him and he knew too, with a dreadful clammy knowledge, that they were out to get him. He glanced wildly in the direction of the people on the distant summit, but a heavy cloud had settled there like a pillow of dense smoke and the people were quite hidden. He began wildly scrabbling along the ridge, shaking and trembling as he went, and then the cats all popped up again, as if at a command, this time very near indeed and with eyes the size of saucers. They crept and padded almost within touch of him; peered down at him, glared up at him, from all directions and at all levels, watching him as he cowered on a narrow ledge, gazing wildly from cat to cat. Then they vanished again. But now he could feel their electric presence closing in upon him and he knew that when next he saw them they would all be pouncing together. He tried to hurry, faster, faster, but there were impassible rocks above him and on either side and plunging space beneath him. He clung wildly to hard, uncaring rock, his sandalled feet sliding on small scree which here covered the so-called track. He could not bear the suspense of waiting for the cat faces again; he yelled, 'Shoo!' to the

* It is called Striding Edge because it is so narrow that a man is supposed to be able to sit astride it.

124

emptiness round him and heard his voice echo back from the cliffs towering on his right. Again he shrieked, 'Shoo!' and waited, sweating and trembling, for the cats to show themselves. Had he scared them away? Too much to hope for! Yet where were they? He edged himself up a little and then they were all there, crouched ready to spring, their eyes large as dinner-plates.

And he shouted in a loud voice, 'I won't steal no more cats! I won't steal no more cats!' and the echoes repeated it back and forth from Nethermost Pike to Catstycam. But the animals seemed not to hear; they peered down at him and up at him and from every side upon him and not one eye blinked or whisker twitched amongst them.

He saw their haunches tighten, ready to launch them upon him; he gave one more piercing cry of 'Shoo!' and jerked on the rock, slipped and, with a terrible shout that rang among the crags, plunged head first into the mists stirring over the tarn.

The cats craned forward, staring down into the nothingness of the mists, hearing the echoes of Pike's last cry roll round them and then die, hearing the boulders that he had dislodged as he fell bound and crash and rattle after him.

Then all was utter silence.

The cats, without a word, began rapidly pacing, leaping and racing back along Striding Edge. They moved faster and faster, never looking over their shoulders. Above Helvellyn thunder rumbled and big drops of rain started to spatter on the rocks that the cats bounded over. Then the storm broke; thunder crashed, lightning stabbed and zig-zagged, rain streamed down in cataracts and, striking the rocks, exploded upward in jets of flying water. The cats, now terrified, were quickly soaked to the skin. Lollia Paulina found herself panting along, clutching Goofer's paw. The lightning cracked in blue freak-outs of fire and the thunder pealed against each crack. At last the cats reached the wall; there the terriers lay sheltering squeezed in a heap, trembling and whining. The cats squeezed alongside them. Here all the animals remained until the storm was over. Then they got up, stretched themselves, shook themselves and raced home down the mountainside as if some ghost were at their heels.

Back at the grotto they dried themselves and had something to eat and catnip to drink and presently they felt warm again and were able to talk, even to laugh. Nobody mentioned Wilberforce. Then Hamish took out his pipes and started to compose a pibroch: 'Fear not the thunder . . .' and Pooks rattled on his drum and Ranjit Singh sang a Sikh hymn to victory and stamped and bristled his tail and hissed and growled and then he did his famous cobra-dance and leapt up and down and spun round and round so fast that he became only a blur. He twiddled faster and faster and faster and Goofer Sahib, who was sitting next to the Lollypop in a trance-like state of bliss, stretched out his legs without realizing that he was stretching out his legs, and Ranjit Singh caught his foot in them and shot clean across the lawn like a bullet and crashed head-first into Pooks and his drum, splitting the drum-skin with a deafening roar. And Ranjit Singh picked himself up and stood very straight to attention and said, 'There is thunder in the hills, Scoop Sahib.' And then he fell flat on his back and had to be put to bed with an ice-bag on his head and kept very quiet in the dark for the next twenty-four hours.

While Manx was attending to the mongoose Nibs and Nosher, weary and pad-sore, came limping in. From Nibs's jaws dangled limply all that was left of Sergeant Fleaby, while Nosher carried the General in one side of his mouth and the Colonel in the other. The two cats dropped the motionless rats on to the ground and Nosher said, 'They're all dead and the old gal's fled.'

And Oliver said, 'And the old-red-sprouter has fallen off the mountain.'

'Fallen to where?' asked Nibs.

'To his doom,' said the cats who had seen Wilberforce fall. 'To his doom.'

And there was a great celebration which lasted three days. Cats from all over the kingdom came. They brought laurel-wreaths for victory, which they hung round the necks of the Power Station cats and Watt Tyler and they gave bouquets of wild roses and orchids to Lollia Paulina and Selina, and at dusk orange and yellow lanterns were lit and suspended from the trees so that the celebrating might continue all night.

The terriers, seeing all these cats arrive, made polite little speeches of thanks and farewell, loaded their huge bag of biscuits and sheeps' heads on to a goat and marched off into the fells, with Hamish piping, Brat Wilson driving the goat, Pooks drumming his mended drum and all the rest barking like mad.

Sebastian had to go home to his Miss Pringle, but she promised him that if he were good he might visit Lollia Paulina each summer on a long visit when his friends were there; for the Lollypop had made the Power Station cats swear that they would spend every summer with her.

Watt Tyler was adamant that Oliver should return to the Robinson family. 'We can't have a promising young cat like you turning into a tearaway.' Oliver resigned himself to the idea of respectability. Scratch encouraged him to return to the Robinsons. 'Arter all, we'll make good sure we see plenty of you, mate. Lots, in fact. You'll come up 'ere every summer, same as us lot do, an' we'll see you for weekends at the Power Station, too.'

Manx Scoop wrote a great story about the victory over the rats and the fall of Wilberforce Pike. All the Power Station cats had their pictures on the front pages of the cat-kingdom's newspapers and discovered to their amazement they were saviours of society, splendid young animals, a fine example to the youth of Catdom, and the rest of it. Goofer Sahib was offered a splendid job as director of the Royal Feline Save the Kittens Fund, also as organizer of the Marquis of Purr's Adventure Scheme for Young Cats. He was, too, invited to be Leader of a large new Kitten Club sponsored by the Dowager Duchess of Mouser. He furthermore received twenty-two proposals of marriage from female cats he had never even heard of; some obviously wealthy (you could tell from their note-paper) and others undoubtedly pretty, if one could rely upon the photographs which they enclosed. But the Goofer refused all these offers: he married Lollia Paulina and settled with her by the lake amongst the mountains instead. Selina also remained as companion to the Princess.

They were visited by their friends, the Power Station cats,

including Oliver and Sebastian, every summer, and Watt Tyler came too whenever he could get away from his duties, and the terriers called and they all danced and sang under the stars and, it goes without saying, everyone lived happily ever after.

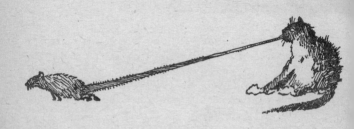